Night Desk

NIGHT DESK

a
novel by
GEORGE RYGA

copyright ©1976 George Ryga

published with assistance from the Canada Council

Talonbooks
201 1019 East Cordova
Vancouver
British Columbia V6A 1M8
Canada

This book was typeset by Linda Gilbert of B.C. Monthly
Typesetting Service, designed by David Robinson and
printed by Web Offset for Talonbooks.

Editor: Karl Siegler

Second printing: October 1977

Canadian Shared Cataloguing in Publication Data

Ryga, George, 1932—
    Night desk
    ISBN 0-88922-089-1 pa.

    1. Title.
    PS8585.Y393N53   C813'.5'4   C76-016035-X
    PR9199.3.R

33,280

for Nikolai,
wherever you are

prologue

He came into my life, stayed for a winter, and vanished. No, that's not true. It was I who vanished from *his* world. I left it at a run, a bundle of manuscripts under my arm. And a headful of memories I have wrestled with all these years. I fled into the university, searching for shelter and the safety of refined literature of other lands, where human affairs are orderly and predictable. Where lecturers spoke to students in words and metaphors never heard on a dusty prairie roadside, or in mining towns where all hope has a coating of grime. In time, the students spoke like their teachers. We were expected to, and obliged our tutors by writing theses on Renaissance poetry, the Restoration novel. Even on the effects of the American Civil War on the literature of the new world.

It was, and continues to be, academic rubbish. But it was warmth and security, and kept us from facing a bare-fanged, gaunt reality moving like wind shadows across the landscape of the country.

I had fled from the night desk and from the towering presence of a man who harangued, terrified and excited me in ways I still cannot describe, but I never fully escaped him.

Strangely fearful of losing his words and gestures, I carried with me the manuscripts I feverishly wrote during that winter. I had virtually memorized all I had written, yet I was haunted by a fear that once they were stolen, or burned, they would somehow be likewise destroyed in my memory. Like a damnation, I heard them laugh in that massive voice of his at the intellectual games, the smoothly turned phrases, the self-indulgences of borrowed life and experiences which in time would have to be repaid — with what? With the impressions of a barren non-existence?

But somewhere in this also lay my salvation. For he was the raucous guardian of the gate to fields of thistles, stones, hunger.

He never called me by my name. His name was important to him, and he restated it at every opportunity. I was simply called "kid". When I knew him, I had yet to earn my name. Until I did, I had the protection of his. This I now understand. As I understand now I must return to the beginning of things to find my own integrity — an integrity he offered to me with a smile on his face and tears trickling from his eyes. An offer I refused in the most profound fear I have ever known. A cowardly refusal, which all the trappings of scholarly accomplishments cannot erase or alter.

Gleaning through this portion of the manuscript I wrote so quickly that long winter many years ago, I blush with the realization that despite many published articles on the craft of communion through the written word, I am a better copiest than I am a creator of fantasy and wonder. For in truth, there is much in this story I still do not understand. There are passages which upset me, and others which make me chafe at the futility of my own existence.

I am in the story somewhere, but not through choice or design. I was only drawn into the vortex, as were others, of his consuming restlessness. He gave what he had freely. I tried to take only that which was useful or fascinating to me. It was a futile exercise, and I quickly realized my time would be better served by recording him, even if the work I was employed to do at the hotel was neglected.

It was. There were two of us dismissed that April morning. Myself, and a bartender who stole seventy dollars from the till. The bartender returned the money in exchange for a letter of recommendation and the dropping of possible charges against him. I did not return to ask for support in finding employment elsewere. I did not think Romeo Kuchmir would have approved of such an act of humiliation. I already felt his disapproval in other things, so I moved as quickly as I could towards the opposite horizon.

one

I went to the ballet at eight o'clock. Yes sir, I went to the ballet tonight!

Does that surprise you? I'm not a barrel of water . . . or a stack of hay. I'm a man! An' I want the best for myself, an' the same for you. So I dress up in my grey suit, polish my shoes an' go to the ballet to sit among women who smell like a flower garden dyin' of frost . . .

Let me tell you about it, kid. But then, how can I tell you a ballet? You can't tell it, or sing it . . . you've got to *dance* it! I could dance it for you if you liked, but then there'd be parts missing . . . an' the garden smell of dyin' flowers would be gone . . . an' that's somehow part of it too.

There's this little Italian broad called Juliet. She can't make it out of this garden, so she swallows some poison. The same with the guy she's goin' around with. They're in bed, but they're not doin' anything in bed together — they're never gonna be able to. That's sad. An' that's what's beautiful . . . they can't do nothin' because they're *dead*. The women sitting around me start heating up. Itchin' in their seats. But the smell they give off is like a funeral. Because it's *their* fault, an' the fault of Juliet's goddamned family, an' the fault of the family of the kid she's goin' around with. Everyone knows healthy kids got to run an' play an' screw when they get the chance. If they don't, they're gonna die, an' it's somebody's fault . . . always somebody's fault.

I went to the ballet at eight o'clock, an' I cried until half-past nine. The last time I did that was when my mother died, may the angels give her wings that never wear out. She was a good woman, even after she married my father.

He killed her, you know. The old bastard ran a poolhall in a small town that's since been eaten up by Calgary. In the evenings he'd stand around with his hands in his pockets keeping young punks from lifting the table felts with their cue sticks.

"Hey, weasel-face! This is expensive property! You remember that, or I'll kick your butt into your shoulders!" He spoke like that when he was feelin' good an' was being nice to the kids.

He also sold french safes under the counter to any boy having trouble with his root. For an extra dollar, he'd fix it up so the kid could get in the backdoor of Sweet Mabel's place. Sweet Mabel ran a candy store with a one-woman cathouse in the back. She'd let a man in the way he was an' for nothin' because "they know the proper thing to do." But young punks taking the dip for the first or second time had to have the swelling packed in rubber.

"They go off all over the place, an' some of them got eczema," she says to me once. "I handle candy for the kids. I can't risk spreading eczema."

When my old man wasn't at the poolhall, he was home. I mean he was at *home* — like a big stone in the garden, or a boil on your ass. Nothing moved him. She had to lift his feet to sweep around his chair. She had to cook, clean, plant a garden, clear the snow. For he was Fedyor Kuchmir, descendant of the Don Cossacks. An' when he talked to me, which wasn't often, he told me his ancestors had cut off heads of Turks.

"When you gonna cut off a Turks' head?" I asked him one day in the winter when both of us stood at the window in the warm kitchen watching her outside, up to her knees in snow, splitting wood for the fire.

"When it sticks up high enough to get in my way," he said.

He had shoeboxes full of medals. When he pinned

them on, he looked like Herman Goering. They came from service clubs where he drank whiskey an' made loud speeches about how much he loved the queen of England. He made it as a mayor once . . . yeah. The same time Sweet Mabel was elected to the council. She got her sidewalk paved, the decision for that being made the night of November 15th, 1957, when she invited the mayor an' three men on the council to her back room for a vote.

Here kid, this is a sports coat an' three shirts I want you to put through for overnight cleaning. Put a note to tell them not to starch the collars. There's bums workin' in the laundries now would put starch in socks. An' they got hair like women. The world's fillin' up with men who never cut their hair!

Some of them work in restaurants as cooks. I once ordered a doughnut an' a cup of coffee in a cafe up the street. A little broad with blue eyes two tables down does the same. The waitress brings both our orders an' sets them down. The little broad picks up her doughnut an' puckers to bite it. Mine slides off my plate. I grab for it, an' it jerks the other one out of the little broad's mouth. We're friends now, connected by a seven-foot long hair cooked into our doughnuts an' strong as piano wire! I move to her table, believin' as I do god has more ways than four of bringin' a woman to a man.

Put the cleaning on my bill. If you've got a Saskatchewan pig farmer stayin' in the hotel, put it on his bill. Pig farmers don't argue over hotel bills. There's only so low a man sinks before his suffering is silent.

How much do I owe? . . . Look it up, then. There's somethin', somewhere, written down about every man who lives. Half the bible was written around Moses. A man like me has to settle for a laundry an' hotel bill.

That much, eh? You haven't heard them say anything about planning to evict me? Naw, don't tell me — don't depress me.

I've been around this hotel on an' off for fifteen years. Came here the first time in the back of a second-hand hearse, six other wrestlers an' me. The guy drivin' the hearse was old Ross, the promoter. Built like a brick shithouse an' dumb as he was big. We used to wrestle in towns with only one grain elevator, times were that bad. One night seven of us wrestled for five people. Ross gave us two-bits an' an apple each for our work that night!

I've been poor, kid, but never down. I left Ross when I seen him fight a city bus. He was crossin' Jasper Avenue, just two blocks down from here. Along comes this diesel bus an' boom! It hits Ross. Ross picks himself off the street, hits himself here an' there to check for broken bones — nothin! He's in good shape. But the front of the bus is caved in an' the windshield busted. Any other day, that might've been that. But the bus driver is the kind who don't even let a cripple ride for free.

"Why in hell don't you watch where you're goin', farmer?" he hollers at Ross. Which was the wrong thing to do.

Ross shakes himself, stares at the driver an' the bus, spits an' takes a run at it. He hits the side of the bus with his shoulder. It rocks from side to side like a cradle. People inside are screamin' an' climbing over one another to get out. The driver goes out the window an' hightails it out of there. Other passengers have now kicked out emergency escape windows an' are pouring out like wild cattle from a broken corral. Because old Ross is now poundin' the bus to crap, putting dents into it, smashing windows with his elbows.

Fellows with small brains are meaner than guys with big brains once they get worked up. That's why I don't like fascists. I knew a Polish fascist who beat his dog to death with a shoe when he'd heard on the radio that Hitler had lost the war.

"Hey — quit it!" I hollered at old Ross. "The fuzz will

14

arrest you for bus slaughter. That's enough!"

The old prick stopped and turned to glare at me an' the other wrestlers he had workin' for him.

"Useless, no-good grub sacks!"

An' he's charging us, like a bull, head first. By now we'd all had our problems with Ross. Being driven like dead meat from town to town in his goddamned hearse was one thing — no money was another. An' we were young an' horny, needin' women in the worst sort of way, but all he'd given us was draught. A good promoter looks after his boys. Kids need lollipops — grown men need nooky! So we beat him up. Just before we knocked him out, with four of us holdin' him up an' three others punchin' the hell out of him, we told him we'd quit. Then we put him out an' stuck him behind the wheel of his hearse. One of the wrestlers with a sense of humour put a cigarette in old Ross' mouth an' straightened his necktie. Then we took his wallet containin' twenty-eight dollars, which we split seven ways an' took off to make our fortunes in this world.

Yeah, I've been poor . . .

Before you worked here, years ago, I only had one suit of clothes to my name. I'd come down like I done tonight, to leave my clothes for overnight cleaning. Only then when I came down I was wearin' nothing but my undershorts.

There used to be a drunk sleeping in that chair by the door. A funny old bastard with a sheepskin cap on his head, flaps tied down under his chin like an immigrant from Peru. Looked like Father Christmas with no teeth. One night I'm down here, talkin' to the night clerk who worked here before you. Another old tit who'd fought in the first war an' could never stop serving. He was a company man an' a drunk himself, but that's another story . . . Anyway, I'm breezin' with Sam — Sam was his name — an' the guy with the sheepskin cap in the chair starts to sing:

"Oh, the cow kicked Nellie in the belly in the barn . . ." he sings.

15

"Go back to sleep, old timer," I says to him. "Your train's left the station. Next one in comes through at four . . ."

I'm just joshin' him along. He's harmless an' I'm feeling well disposed to anythin' smaller than me.

"Thank you, captain," an' he kind of bowed to me like I was somebody important. Almost fell out of the chair doing it. Then he sort of twitches up an' slaps the leather arms of the chair with both hands.

"Oh, the cow kicked Nellie . . ."

That's as far as he got with singin', for it petered out into a kind of bubbling snore, his head fallin' to one side, his toothless mouth opening in a dumb grin. I tapped him nicely on the cheek, for he wasn't anything you wanted to look at while believin' man could aspire to somethin' beyond this life.

"Hey, old timer!" I says.

He's awake, his small eyes starin' at nothing, his mouth chewin' on itself. "Yeh?"

"How come you wasn't born a general . . . or a waiter in a french cafe? I ask him. He grins at me and points his finger at my crotch.

"You got no pants . . . You is bare-assed nekkid, boy!" An' he pokes me with a mittened finger in the dink. Then he's up on his feet, slappin' his hands and twitchin' his shoulders, laughin', singing his way out into a thirty-below night:

"Oh, the cow kicked Nellie in the belly in the barn . . ."

You know, there are men, an' women in this hotel an' other places I know, who ask about you. An' I tell them. I tell 'em, "The kid on the night desk is writin' down what we do an' say — about who we are an' what we might've been. The trumpet of the night. That's what you are." Don't be surprised or frightened. Praise me or condemn me. I'll protect you. You're all we have between us an' the grave.

When you write about this time an' the way we were,

do me a favor, kid. Ask the world a question — one question. Ask why some poor woman long ago pooched herself inside out to give birth to that old punk who sat in that chair, when she might've popped a saint. Or a jet pilot. Ask why, an' if someone tells you, but I'm dead by then, you go find my grave an' you dig a hole until you reach my ear. An' when you've dug the earth out of my earhole with your finger, you holler loud the answer so I can sleep forever, happy that I know everything!

I seen a ballet at eight o'clock tonight. They danced it for me — only me. Because I was on fire — my face an' hair in flames, begging for the truth of who died an' why so that I might avenge them!

Anyway, that other night when I was here in the lobby dressed in nothin' but my undershorts, two old women came through the street door. Before I could run, they seen me. I had to act. I'm an actor — a performer. A good one.

"Look at me! Look at what a burglar did!" I shouted, tears comin' to my eyes an' the old bum soldier of a night desk clerk rushing for a towel to wrap around my ass.

"I'm an honest man. I believe in god an' god's mother an' all the angels an' saints he's got workin' for him. I'm an honest man. I sleep like an honest man: my door unlocked, my wallet on the table, my shoes beside the door. I'm sleepin', dreaming of my mother — god protect her from the rain! A burglar comes into my room. He takes everything I own, ladies! My shirt, my pants, my socks, my wallet, a photograph of my wife an' children, my prayerbook! Here I stand before you, ladies, forty-seven years old an' naked as the day I was born! Another man — a burglar, a child of god like myself, did it to me!"

When I'm finished, those two mothers, one short, one tall, one ugly an' the other homely, each took five dollars from their handbags an' handed the money over to me. Such is the power of the word!

"Sir," the taller one says, "we're sorry about what

happened. We work with retarded children an' the pay is little. But we hope this will help to restore your confidence in mankind!''

I took the money. Oh, I kissed the hands offering it to me an' ran upstairs. I went to bed an' lay there, trembling. I was guilty, but I could also see the possibilities of a new career. Any punk with half a brain can trade or sell a house, a wheelbarrow or a wet puppy. But to exchange human yearnings for cash — *that* was something else! As I'm sweating, turnin', thinkin' of these things, my telephone rings. It's the desk clerk, an' he wants a cut of the money.

"Stretch out an' die! You scurvied dog!" I yell at him. "I went to their rooms an' gave the money back — how does that grab you?"

He had nothin' to say, but I kept shoutin' at him, squeezin' the telephone until I heard it crack an' then crumble in my hand.

"Nothin's black an' white," I says to him. "Life's not like that. Life's as grey as a thousand miles of prairie in the winter, an' you're a one-eyed gopher staring at a black thistle an' thinking you've just seen a pillar ten miles high!"

I'm an outlaw, kid, a stallion. I'm goin' where I'm goin' an' no one asks me why.

After I seen that ballet tonight, I says to myself, "I've got to keep screwin' because I'm alive, an' because it feels good an' because I don't want to die an' smell like a flower garden in November . . ."

What makes some women missionaries an' others hookers, do you know? Sometimes I think there's no difference. They're both the same. It's got somethin' to do with the need to serve. Don't laugh, kid. I'm serious. I know you're a good catholic boy, but you'll outgrow it. If you don't, all that scribblin' you're doing won't save your soul or mine, an' I'll stand behind you all the way.

Here's somethin' else for you to think about: when I

was a kid your age, I had a cousin called Stella, who took to religion like a calf takes to the milk bucket. I was a big muscled village punk, razzin' cops, breathin' heavy when my old man got too near. Family didn't like me. Called me corrupt. After Stella, they disowned me. Called me a degenerate.

And because I, Romeo Kuchmir, was ruined, Stella saw herself as my redeemer, ready to bring me back on the road to salvation.

One summer afternoon, we went for a walk. Past town, through fields of barley, down to the river where a lot of willows grew. At first we weren't sayin' much, but in the willows, she starts pleadin' with me to cut the booze an' broads, get myself together, let god an' her be my friends. While she talked like that, I started takin' off my clothes. I flexed my muscles an' danced around her — kind of slow at first, but building up steam as I went along. She had to keep turnin' to follow me, her little ass twisting this way an' that, because she wore high heels an' the ground was soft.

In a big but helpless voice I says to her, "It's no use." I was the devil, except in one place, where god was tryin' to get out. "See how he's pushin'," I shouted at her, "see how he's pushin', he's tryin' to get out but he can't!"

"Get hold of his door-handle, Stella!"

She's bug-eyed with fear, but she reaches out an' gets hold of my root. First with one hand, then with two . . .

"That's it!" I holler. "That's it! The devil's got me, an' god's tryin' to get out — Help him!"

Jesus, Jesus — she's sayin', an' pretty soon she's not afraid no more. She's got my wang in both hands, an' while I'm dancin' around her, she's pushin', pullin', twistin', laughin', like a kid with a new red wagon. Then she's down on her knees, dizzy, her face red, her eyes dreamin' . . .

I didn't tell anyone, but Stella, well, I don't know because she got sent to Africa by her group. An' my uncle

Nick an' my father both told me to get my ass out of the house an' family an' never come back again. My mother? Well, she didn't say anything. She only looked worried when all this happened, but she never said a word to me one way or the other . . .

But that's not what I started to tell you, no. What I wanted to say is what started as a bit of crackerjack down by the river became a religious experience for me. I've never forgotten it. I've never asked Stella or anyone for forgiveness, because I've never felt what happened there was bad or hurtful.

two

You sweep the lobby floor even when it's clean — why? It's not the shiny floor or the polish on the desk that brings me down to talk to you. It's the feel of men, the sound of things not said.

Look at the clock — it's after midnight. I just got one day older, kid — one day nearer to my death. It's the same for you, even if you try to sweep away the truth off an empty floor. The bricks an' waterpipes know. The wind knows. The stars know.

I've been readin' what you wrote here while you were upstairs checking for fires an' whores. Perhaps what you say is pretty good, but who am I to tell? I'm not an educated man. I can't read truth — I smell it! What you have there has a feeble smell, but in time, who knows?

I'd give my last shirt to an honest man. I'd *give* it! But how many have come to take it without asking? I don't like that, an' I'm not talkin' about burglars. If a burglar comes into my room, I'll take care of him — I'm no cripple, an' I weigh two hundred an' fifty pounds. But crooks with words scare me. The ones who come into my life with talk of love an' brotherhood. The ones who write up papers which take my land away from me or my kids. The worst kinds — men an' women — are the ones who rob me of my feelings, who can persuade me that love is business, that the poor should be grateful Jesus died for them! That everything I feel an' say is selfish. That I will never rise above the level of a mindless animal!

I don't like that, kid. Don't ever write that about me. For when I read, I read aloud, my fingers following the

lines, every word an enemy unless it makes me laugh —
or cry!

Do you sing?

Ah, kid — you should learn to sing. It's the sound of
blood welcoming the sun! I was born with a lump of happiness jammed into my throat — listen!

La donna mobile . . .

Try it! . . . No, not like that! It's got to start down in
the balls an' if you turn your face up, it hits the clouds an'
brings down rain! Put away your pen an' the ledgers of the
thieves who own this place. I'll give you a drink of whiskey
in my room an' we'll go out into the street an' sing — you
an' I! It's twenty-five below out there. Will this winter
ever really end if we don't sing?

I know good singers. Jan Peerce is a friend of mine. We
were punks together long ago, in cheap hotels from San
Francisco to Dallas. Me wrestlin', him singin'. Once, on the
coast of Maine, we walked together through a storm, both
singin' arias from Puccini. He forgot the words, but *I*
remembered them. Hey, but we sang! The wind an' rain
howlin' in from the cold Atlantic . . . an' there was Peerce
an' me, bent into the wind, singin' for the broads asleep
with other men. But that's alright, the silent ones are
brothers too.

He came to Edmonton in November. You were off that
night. He sends a ticket to me, an' I go to hear him. But he
didn't make me happy. I came back drunk I was that mad.
Jan Peerce is dead — I don't know him! He's a fat prick
now, singin' for the rich an' dumb. He knew it — I'd gone
backstage to tell him.

"Take your 'Bluebird of Happiness' an' shove it up your
ass, amigo," I says to him. "Romeo Kuchmir came all the
way across town to hear you, an' you betrayed me. I didn't
hear Jan Peerce. I heard a three-grand-a-night punk doin'
exercises. I've heard you singin' better warmin' up in a
baggage car on the way to Tulsa. Here's half your ticket

22

back. I just wasted the other half they tore off to let me in!"

So I get back here an' go to bed. He phones me from the MacDonald, the hotel with class. He don't stay in workingmen's hotels no more.

"Romeo," he says, "I'm sorry about tonight. I want to make it up to you. Get over an' we'll kill a bottle of scotch together, for the sake of old times, buddy."

"Fall down a shithole," I says to him. "To make up for tonight, it'll cost you *two* bottles of scotch an' you're comin' *here* to drink it. Right here, where the fire system don't work, an' people still screw an' hit each other like they once did."

He came. An' we got drunk together. An' we talked about the old days, an' how we sang together on the coast of Maine. An' then we cried a little about time passing, an' what had happened to us. I stopped cryin' first. He cried a bit longer, which made me think he was worse off than me.

There was this little woman long ago. She played piano in country towns with two grain elevators an' one poolhall. She played a Brahms recital in my town, what a night that was! It was winter outside, snow two feet deep, car exhausts steaming. But inside there was summer, with joy, green trees, cattle grazing on stone-speckled pastures. Learn to sing, kid, or at least learn to play music even if it's no more than bangin' a pot lid to the rhythm of your heart.

La donna mobile . . .

You ever been in love? Still too young, is that it?

You're never too young. I fell in love with that pianist when I was nine. I was ten when I got laid the first time. Not by the same woman. The one who screwed me was the wife of the telegraph operator who worked in Red Deer an' only came home for three days at the end of each month.

I was runnin' home from a softball game one evening.

23

I knew I was late. Instead of followin' the road, I crossed some fields an' gardens, tryin' to get home the shortest way. In one vacant lot, I run into some nettles, which burned my legs as I was wearing short pants. Through a fence, an' I'm crossin' this small yard surrounded by high caragana hedge. An' sittin' on the back porch, naked to the waist, combing her hair, was this woman — the wife of the telegraph operator. The first thing I seen was these large white tits, scooping out like two plow-beams. Then I look up an' see her starin' at me, her face shaded by her hair.

"What are you doin' here?" she asks, her voice low an' soft. I couldn't say a thing. I couldn't get my eyes off her tits with the pink nipples which reminded me of little rosebuds.

"What are you lookin' at?"

"Nothin'," I lied.

"Come here . . . How old are you?"

"Sixteen," I lied again.

She put her comb down an' got out of her chair to put on a small jacket, which she closed an' held with one hand. It made me sad to see her do that.

"What's your name?"

"Fred Kuchmir." I gave her my father's name. She looked at me a long time, an' then she sort of looked past me, an' her face made me think she might cry.

"Would you like an apple? I got some fresh raisin pie too."

In her livingroom I was eatin' an apple an' scratchin' the backs of my legs against the rough couch. She sat on the coffee table in front of me. In one hand she held an apple, which she ate quickly. With the other, she held the front of her jacket closed. She was holdin' it very tight, the knuckles showin' white.

Then like she was reachin' for another apple for herself, she began to touch and squeeze me between the legs. Another kid my age might've dropped his apple an' run.

I almost did, at first. But then somethin' inside me started to bloom an' heat up, like the sun comin' over a hill. I was scared, I sure was, but I couldn't run. She put her arm around me an' pulled my little short pants down. I dropped my apple an' grabbed hold of her ears in both my hands.

We laughed, we wrestled, off the coffee table an' down on the floor. The nettle burns on my legs began to itch an' burn like hell itself, spreadin' up an' all over me. Then she had me inside herself an' she was heavin' an' sighing.

"Peter! . . . Oh, Peter . . . do it . . . DO it!"

Which was strange to me then, because my name wasn't Peter. It was Romeo, same name I have now, but I was only a kid — what did I know about these things? Then I had my first explosion, every cell in my body lettin' go, an' suddenly, I was very sad an' tired an' scared, like I was dyin'.

"Jesus, mother!" I remember sayin', an' she pushed me off her an' I fell to the floor, coverin' my head with my hands. After a while, I looked up at her, an' she was sitting up beside me, almost naked and shiverin', her head bowed between her knees. Then she straightened up an' looked at me, an' I seen the same fear an' sadness in her eyes that I felt in myself. I crawled towards her, an' she bent down an' kissed me on the forehead.

"Go home now — quickly, boy," she whispered. "And don't tell anybody about coming here, not ever!"

There are people who sit watchin' through the peephole of life. The snow falls an' piles up on their heads, but they don't move. They just sit, watchin'. As you're watchin' me, kid. Go ahead — watch! I'm a performer! I bleed, spit out teeth, I howl an' I laugh! You can't touch me! I will lie, an' I will tell the truth, but you will never know the difference. Because you're a watcher!

Come on — don't look at me that way. I'm sorry if I hurt you. It's not you. I'm talkin' through you to the dead

25

souls with pension plans an' homes of their own. You're closer to me than my mother. I live through you. Tell me to go away an' I'll go. But if I'm stayin', then I'm here to make you my mouth, my fist, my cock!

I promoted a wrestling match last year in the building where they keep livestock for the horse an' cow shows — you know the place — east end of the city. The place smells of shit an' popcorn.

The wrestlers I hired were old an' fat. Two of them were senile. I had no bread, so I took what nobody wanted. I put these two dumbos into a warmup event. They each took a fall, then became confused. They couldn't find each other, so one took on the referee, the other a corner post of the ring, which he eventually broke off. I had to throw them out. The match was a disaster, a comedy show. I figured makin' half a grand, but all I cleared was seventy dollars an' thirty-five cents!

After the match I rented the big room here for a party. Laid on some fried chicken an' beer for the boys. But these old timers wanted broads.

"Chicken an' beer are on me, you guys. Anything else you pay for!" I says to them.

"Yah . . . yah . . . sure . . ."

An' they started phonin'.

In half an hour, the whores were comin' in. Like they'd been dumped by a truck in front of the hotel. Bargain basement jobs with clap, bad teeth, sore feet. Except one — Margo, who come in last an' who didn't belong. She was in a different class, but times were tough.

I knew her, not as a whore, but as someone from my childhood. There was a teacher in the school I went to when I was a kid, a Missus Dayton, who was widowed or divorced an' had two little girls with her. Margo was the youngest.

Missus Dayton was sick a lot of the time. She'd have headaches which lasted three, four days at a stretch. She'd close the school when she was sick an' we'd go home. Next day we'd go back an' return home, because she wasn't there. Margo an' her sister, they hung around town a lot during summer holidays, always together, an' I thought a lot about them. I thought that maybe they'd be hungry when she was sick because if she was too sick to teach she was too sick to cook. I was a funny kind of kid, things like that bothered me. An' I'd feel sorry for them. That comes from my mother. She always felt sorry for the poor.

Mushrooms an' morels grew pretty good in those places where river birch an' poplars shaded the ground in summer. As a kid, I kept our house in mushrooms from June to September. My mother dried a few varieties for winter soup, which was black as ink when she cooked it. It had a sharp, peppery taste. I never had a cold when I ate that soup.

I worried a lot about Margo, her sister an' Missus Dayton that summer. But anyone can worry, it takes a kid with mushroom experience to do somethin' about the worry. So one Sunday mornin', I'm off with two metal pails in my hands. It's rainin', a soft rain which hangs in the trees an' on the grass, a perfect day for mushrooms. I picked the best there was — not a wormhole in any of them. I even washed the stems in the creek, somethin' I'd never done before. In the afternoon my clothes were soaking, an' my feet an' hands were scratched, but I got me two pails of the finest mushrooms in the country that day.

I could see the two kids an' Missus Dayton through the front window of their house as I approached the door an' knocked. The teacher comes to the door. Her face is white an' old lookin'. I could tell she was sick again.

"I picked them for you," I says, holdin' out the two pails of mushrooms. She looks at them, then at me. Somethin' was wrong, she wasn't sure . . .

"Do . . . you people eat this?" she asks.

"Huh?"

By now, the two kids are beside her. They looked hungry an' worried.

"Do . . . Ukrainians eat these?"

"Sure, all kinds of people eat mushrooms. Cows eat 'em too!" I says.

"You've eaten them yourself?"

"Yep."

"Then perhaps you had better take them home for your mother," she says, blinkin' with the pain in her head.

"No. They're for you . . ."

"I don't want them. I'm sorry!" Her voice gets high an' sharp all of a sudden. I'm still a kid. I don't know what to do, so I hold up the pails to her. She takes them an' marches down the steps an' to the corner of the house where a small lilac bush is growin'. She lifts the pails one at a time an' empties them around the roots of the bush. Then she kicks some dead grass an' rotten leaves over them an' hands me back the empty pails.

Like I say, I knew Margo before she was a hooker. Seein' her now, her teeth needin' repairs an' her shoulders hunched, I feel more sorry for her than ever. There's somethin' in her eyes that's still alive, but the clothes she's wearin' are worn an' look as if they'd been slept in. Her hair's not cut, an' has the sweaty look of someone who's not eatin' too good. A third-rate hooker. I take her aside an' out into the hallway.

"Margo," I says.

"Who in hell you talkin' to? My names' not Margo. My name's Millie!" She snaps an' moves away from me.

"Come on, kid. I know you. I knew your mother an' your sister . . ."

She's backed against the wall, as far away from me as she can get. Her eyes have gone hard, her fists clenched.

"Who in hell are you? I don't know you!" I could tell she's about to cry. Then just as quickly, the whore mask comes over her face, an' she's got a grin on, her voice goes soft.

"Look fella, if you're tryin' to get around me for some free tail, forget it. I've got a guy at my house who takes care of that. This place is business, nothin' else!"

I don't care what they say about me, there are things I would never do. I'd never take an orphan girl in out of the snow to feed her an' then screw her. I may be corrupt, but I'm not rotten. What could I say to her? What could I do?

I start walkin' away.

"Who are you? One of them wrestlers?"

"Yeh, a wrestler. Name is Kuchmir, Romeo Kuchmir."

Now she's excited an' angry an' comes at me like a spike into butter. "You're no ball of hot shit yourself, Kuchmir. Your mother did all the work, an' your old man ran a pool-hall, right? You were so poor you walked around in short pants, when other kids had long pants and jackets. Oh yes, I remember you. You were nothin' special! My mom used to say you ate mushrooms that grew on manure piles, you were that poor. An' you're not very smart to end up a wrestler. Wrestlers aren't exactly god's answer to women. I've known all of you, an' none of you are much better than pigs!"

Sayin' all that, she turned an' walked out. Walked out of my party, walked out of this hotel, walked out of my life.

It's not true what she said about wrestlers, kid. A great wrestler's got to be sad . . . an' heroic. The last of the gladiators. A body bigger than ordinary men — trained to fight, to tear the heart out of a livin' bull, to walk across the world, performin' for peanuts an' sandwich money. No place he comes from, an' no place to go. No home or nooky of his own — all he gets belongs to other men, second-hand an' worn out.

Long ago, a hundred of us might've taken on the world, an' won! Today there's motors an' chainsaws an' machine-guns can cut us up like paper.

You know what's sad about all that? What's sad is that
we continue to live. That we've become clowns playin' for
laughs! An' who's laughin' at us? Every prune-prick with
ulcers in his guts an' arthritis in his balls. He's sittin' out
there in the bleachers, laughin', gettin' it off because he's
on top now an' we're on the bottom lookin' up. The same
guys who took away our clubs, our horses, our houses an'
our iron overcoats — they're up there laughin'! With gun-
powder, they shot our swords to shit. They got everybody
votin', an' we were put out to pasture. Watchin' over us in
the pasture at first was a cripple. Then a kid. An' pretty
soon it's gonna be women with theatre school training!

Sure, before long the women are gonna manage us, tell
us when to sleep, what to eat, when to rest, what clothes
to wear, how to speak nice an' how to speak mean. A
hundred years from now, the last laugh will be ours, an'
you know why? Because all the sickies will start to die.
They're dyin' already!

Cancer an' heart attacks an' malaria aren't spreadin'
like the papers say — no sir! What's happening is that
people who should've died as kids, would've died if it
wasn't for vitamins an' antibiotics an' incubators, they're
livin'. They're livin' with death inside of them. There's
more of them now than anybody, making packaged foods,
car accidents an' kids with the same sickness they've got.
I'm healthy, but I've got to live like the sick, think like the
sick, smell like the sick.

It's the advantages they've made that kill them. Kid,
I love the world an' everythin' living on it — especially
people. But I'm afraid, not of nuclear weapons, that's
nothin'. Wars are made for land, cities an' prisoners. Nobody — not even a madman would reduce what he wants
to ashes. No, I'm afraid it'll come from the way we live,
from the panic of the weak an' sick. It won't be hunger
that'll make us look at a camel-driver as a brother, it'll be

some bug or virus no more serious than a bad cold to a goatherd in Syria who's never known anything except hard times. It's dumb, an' there's nothin' we can do about it now.

You know the dumbest thing I ever seen?

I was in Winnipeg . . . winter . . . three o'clock in the morning. Thirty-four below zero with a twenty miles north wind. No cars, no pedestrians within twenty miles of each other. An' there's this old punk standin' at an intersection, freezin' his stub off, waiting for the traffic light to change! I come up behind him, an' liftin' him up by the armpits, carry him across the red light. He kicks an' bitches, so halfway across the street, I let him down. Goddamn if he didn't turn back to where he'd stood. An' he waits there until the light turns green, then starts to cross. I come towards him, laughin'.

"Hey, old timer," I says to him, "what would happen if the light froze an' didn't change all night?"

He's grinnin' and dodgin' to get by me, for I have my arms spread out to catch him an' give the old bastard a hug. I could see he was a flat-faced old Uke, same's me, the solid kind who'd think nothin' of pullin' a plow if his horse fell an' died in the field during the depression.

"If the light froze an' stayed froze the rest of your life — would you stand there like you was made of stone?"

"No. I'd of turned around an' gone home. I'm not the queen of England. If I break the law, I pay a fine!" he says. I grab him an' hold him tight against me.

"The queen of England is our queen," I says to him. "When she learns to ride a moose side-saddle, we'll make her boss of everything!"

"Don't say that!"

"Why not?"

"What in hell are you — a bolshevik?" He was pushin' an' kickin' to get away from me. "If you're a bolshevik, I don't want to know you."

"Come on, what've the bolsheviks done to you?"

"They raped my mother an' took her egg basket!"

When an old man says that in the middle of a Manitoba blizzard, you've got to let him go. He stood in front of me, grinnin', like a shoemaker in paradise.

"My mother was carrying a basket of eggs to the village market in the old country long ago. She bent down to take a pine needle out from between her toes. Two bolsheviks came from behind, an' while she was bent over like that, they raped her, then took her basket of eggs. I'll never forgive them for that."

"When did this happen?"

"Nineteen-fifteen," he says to me.

"Were you there? Did you see it happen? How do you know all that?"

"No. I was born nine months later. But she told me lots of times why I should hate bolsheviks!" The old bugger was still grinnin'. I took him by the back of the neck an' shook him like a pillow as we walked, the icy wind to our backs.

"I had a wife an' a couple of kids," he was tellin' me. "Wife died, kids are grown up. The boy drives a cat for the highways department in Ontario. The girl's a nurse. Nice lookin' kid, but she's got no time for her father — not her. Both kids don't like me very much. When I'm feelin' bad, I walk a lot. An' I drink a bit when I'm feelin' good, and then I like to play cards, for money. A little bit of money — just enough to feel the old excitement warm my bones."

"Do you win at cards?"

"No. Sometimes I lose my whole pension cheque in one night an' then I'm pretty hungry for the rest of the month. But that's alright. At least I've *lived* for a few hours!" he says, an' giggles an' rubs his mittened hands together.

"You dumb old tit! Come on — I'll buy you a drink."

We found a bootlegger who was open night an' day, an' who sold us a bottle of rye an' a bowl of onion soup, which we ate standin' up, holding the bowls in our hands. Then we drank the whiskey. The Winnipeg winter night didn't seem as cold anymore. The old punk was laughin' an' wantin' me to go to his house. But I was tired of his company. I was startin' to burn, an' he was a fire extinguisher.

So I left, walkin' fast, because it was freezin', the wind cutting into my face. He ran after me, cacklin' like a rooster who'd just found three willin' hens.

"Hey, rassler! I've got lots of likker in my house. We could drink until morning. We could drink all day tomorrow!"

"Go away," I holler at him. "You're too timid for me. I don't believe your mother got knocked up by bolsheviks!"

"They made me. What other proof do you need?"

"You weren't made by a bolshevik. You were made by a coward, a wife-beater, a drunkard who played cards for pennies once a month. Go home!"

He got sad an' stopped followin' me. I looked at him an' saw tears in his eyes.

"Teach me to be brave, rassler," he begged.

"C'mere," I wagged my finger an' he approached, his oversized boots shufflin'. I pointed down the windy, grey, frozen street.

"See them parkin' meters, old timer? There's five hundred miles of parkin' meters in Winnipeg."

"Yah."

"They're the law, an' we're the bandits, you an' I, old timer!"

"Yeh — we're the bandits!" He pushed the fur cap back on his head, an' his eyes were bright with excitement.

"Let's piss into the money slots of the parkin' meters an' screw the law by freezin' it until spring."

He was game. We unzipped ourselves, but he was slow an' a born follower. I'd dribbled into five meters, which steamed for a moment, an' then froze solid before he overtook me an' took on the sixth meter. I passed him, my stub in my hand, an' went to the seventh meter an' the eighth.

When I looked back I seen he was emptyin' his bladder into the one meter.

"Hey!" I shouted. "Just a squirt, an' on to the next one. You don't have to fill the pipestand — just a squirt to freeze the mechanism where the money goes in!"

"I can't make it stop! When I start to piss, it just keeps comin'!"

I hit another six meters before I was empty. Zippin' up, I waited for him. He was still at the same meter, soakin' it down, so to speak. He was laughin', an' I was laughin'.

"It feels good, eh?"

"Yeh, it feels good," he says. "We sure pissed the system to a stop, rassler!"

Behind him, a police cruiser turns from a side street. The old punk didn't see it. He was laughin' as he shook the last drops from his pipe. But the two cops inside the car saw him. They threw on the roof light an' the siren an' came screamin' down at him.

"Run!" I hollered, but he couldn't hear me. He just stood there, holdin' his soft old dink in his mittened hands. I slipped into a doorway an' watched them grab an' throw the old punker into the back of the wagon.

I was laughin'. But I also understood why some men should never do things which are against their nature. They're beat before they start, an' nothin' on earth or in heaven will change that . . . nothin' . . .

three

. . . I know who I love
An' I know who I'll marry,
Fairest of them all
Is my handsome, winsome Johnny . . .

The tune to that song is Irish, kid. They're good singers an' makers of songs, the Irish. I didn't sing that right. My voice is too low, it's colored like my skin with a mishmash of Tartars, Mongols, Cossacks. Turks an' blue-eyed northerners that's the bloodstream of the Slav. Every part wantin' to get out of the stream an' go home. There's somethin' sad about a heart that bleeds for an' with everybody, all the races of the world. So we sing dirges in minor key an' low voices.

But not the Irish. A good Irish man who sings does so with the voice of a happy Russian mother!

They're good fighters, mean fighters, but only for a short time. Ring a churchbell an' they're off to confession. A Slav is different. He takes longer to heat up, but when he does, there's no time limit to a fight. He'll fight even when he's got too old to remember why . . .

See this gold-capped tooth? An Irishman broke that in a fight. He was tough, big, with ears like garden shovels. I was laughin' when he hit me. I was still laughin' when he hit me the second time, an' I spat out a tooth. Then I got mad. For five minutes he fought good. Gave me a bloody nose an' a cut across the cheek — you can still see it here. By then I'd made up my mind I'd have to kick the shit out of him. He knew it too . . . I could see it showin' in his eyes. He comes at me again, with both fists an' a knee.

"Fall down, why don't you?" he's shoutin' at me. "I don't want to hurt you any more than this!"

Those were his last words that day. Because I'd got hold of a wooden chair, which I broke across my knee. An' with the legs an' seat in one hand, an' the heavy back slab in the other, I began to soften him up. It took some time, but when I'd finished with him, he was rolled up on the floor, his knees up to his chin an' his hands wrapped around his head, the fingers locked together like steel clamps.

Saint Patrick . . . he wasn't Irish, you know. He was a Bukovinian shoemaker from a small mountain village in the Carpathians. My grandfather knew the village — four barns an' six small houses. Nothin' good ever came from it.

This man who became Saint Patrick was the worst shoemaker in the world. You know how your left shoe is different from your right shoe? This prick didn't, an' made them both the same, because he'd never seen a proper shoe made by anyone before. He also made them big because he wasn't good at trimmin' leather. He made them so big that when the Austrians took the village in a war, they found a pair of these shoes an' developed them into skis. That's how that business of comin' down the snow in the Alps got started! But the Bukovinians were people same's anyone else. They needed shoes, not skids for a snowy day, so they ran the shoemaker out of the country an' waited around for another one to be born. He left for Poland, but even the Poles couldn't use him, so he was told to keep movin'.

There was no welfare in them days, kid. Today, he'd live like a king, maybe even run a restaurant where they cook meat different. You can kill good meat seventeen different ways today, an' still find somebody who'd eat it, providin' you got a fancy name to put on the mess a starvin' dog would avoid!

Take chicken wings. We used to throw chicken wings out

when I was a kid. Who in hell would put up with chewin' dead chickenskin on a bone dipped in honey? Today, I know a hundred guys who'd eat the feathers off the wings if they'd been left unplucked!

It was downhill all the way for this Saint Patrick. He went to Germany, tried for a job tyin' up bundles of flax. But he'd get the sleeves of his coat tied in with the straw. So they fired him. He went to Norway then, or Sweden, where the broads are good-lookin', but men look like they'd been axe-chopped out of blocks of wood. They used him there to walk dogs for the rich. But the pay wasn't much.

Then he hears there's a job open for a saint in Ireland, where it's warmer an' you don't have to know much to live.

When I was a kid an' kicked out of home, I came here, to Edmonton. First home I had in this city was a roomin' house. A room of my own, just a little smaller than the cells of some jails I've done time in, an' it cost me twenty dollars a month. I had to share a crapper an' sink with eight other people. I was lonely. Jesus, I was lonely. All day I'd work at the railway yards, loadin' cement bags into trucks. At night, I'd come into this roomin' house, eat an' go to my room. I'd sit in a chair an' listen to waterpipes, the furnace an' every radio wherever it was playin' in the house.

Bein' lonely makes me horny. I had a hard-on day an' night, like a pick handle. I could hang a wet towel on it for an hour while I thought of how I'd die or have my teeth pulled by a blacksmith, or how my mother might kill my father an' then hang herself in the basement. An' still that thing would stand up. No remorse, no shame, a mind an' life of its own. If a good cock goes into politics one day, I'll vote for it. It don't give up.

There was nobody to help me, kid. The two girls who lived in the roomin' house were school teachers who shared a room with a hot-plate an' kept to themselves. I spoke to one of them — Agnes, in the hallway once.

"Hullo," I says to her in a loud voice. "You want to go to a movie? I'm goin' an' don't mind if you come."

She looked at me like I had one eye an' two cowtits painted on my chest. She don't say nothin', she just walks by me an' out into the street. I go into the kitchen to have my supper of peanut butter sandwiches an' a glass of milk, an' there's two guys from other rooms in the house, eatin' the same thing. I tell them about askin' Agnes to the movie.

"Jesus Chris', boy . . . you're lucky she didn't say yes. They're dykes!" the guy with buck teeth who worked in a barbershop says to me, then laughs, his mouth an' teeth full of bread an' peanut butter. But the other guy at the table starts to argue.

"No sir, they're not dykes. They're from Egremont. I know Egremont. There's no dykes in Egremont!" he says.

"Not anymore there ain't. They're both in Edmonton now!" An' the barber's helper laughs a high whinny, like a young stallion comin' in for a feed of evening oats.

"You're full of shit, Jake," his buddy says in a way a professor with a lot on his mind might speak to a student. "Dykes don't get monthlies. These broads do. I seen some rags they left in the garbage on Friday. There was blood there, like with normal broads. They're not dykes."

Sometimes I run low on bread, but don't mention it to the bandits around this place. Especially the ones who say they're my friends. I've never been lucky with friends. All I gather around me are bandits waitin' for Romeo to trip an' fall on his face. They'd pick my pockets if I broke a leg. Which is alright, because I'd do the same to them!

Like Mark, the head clerk in this place. He's a dumb punk who reads by pointin' at the words with his finger. Dresses in a brown suit, an' then wears a black hat an' white shoes with perforations in 'em. He's a rube, it's written on his face an' back . . . RUBE . . . here comes the rube! Big as a coca-cola sign. He's no good at anythin'. He's too lazy to work, an' too stupid to get by without workin'. So he steals an' pretends he's in charge of staff here, when actually everybody else makes decisions for him, from the maids to the bellhops. So he steals, but only up to his own level, like shakin' down the cigarette machine, pocketin' tips left for maids in rooms. He'd never put his hand in the till, because he can't count, an' is afraid of anyone who can. You got nothin' to fear from Mark, kid.

I know Matt, the manager, good too. He stole another man's wife an' money to buy this hotel. Thirty years ago the prick was a junk dealer. Twice a year, in the spring an' fall he took lame horses an' contaminated army surplus canned food to sell to Indians on the reservations. In summer, on Sundays, he worked a tent revival, with faith healin' on the side. Him an' his "angels of mercy" — four teenaged hookers who'd give arthritic old farm bachelors a rub around the knockers in exchange for what pocket money these jokers carried on them.

They used to do that in four old teepee tents they'd set up back of the big tent, where Matt was scarin' the shit out of the poor with a description of hell that was a bit like the depression of the '30's, with polio an' bushfires thrown in for good measure.

Then we got Clapper, the bell-captain, the prize specimen of the lot! I gave him that name — Clapper, about five years ago. His real name's Willie, but he can't remember that anymore. He's got the sift so bad it's cooked his brain to a prune. He'd die if he ate a hot turkey sandwich with pepper sauce. Even a cup of coffee makes his face red as a railroad signal light.

How'd he get it? I don't know. I've heard he cupped it from a young broad he wanted to marry once, who got it from a Hungarian sailor. But I think he got it from his aunt Trudy, who runs a cigar store about six blocks from here.

She'd put it out to any burglar on his coffee break.

Some years back, I seen Clapper behind this desk, drinkin' a hot cup of tea through a straw. His head was swollen like a balloon, his lips purple, hands shakin' . . .

"What's the matter? You fall into a cement mixer?" I says to him, happy-like, because I was feelin' pretty good. He pulls the straw carefully out of his mouth an' grins, an' I never seen a sadder expression of happiness. His gums were thick, an' his tongue was like a plug of raw liver he was tryin' to chew down.

"Tetracycline, Romeo," he says to me. "I'm allergic to tetracycline."

"He's got an infection in his lungs," dumb Mark, who's standin' beside him, tells me. Now I know the kind of doctors Clapper goes to, an' why. An' when they prescribe tetracycline it's for somethin' lower down than where a man's lungs got a business to be.

"Sure makes a mess of your kisser," I says to Clapper in a concerned kind of voice. He nods, pleased as hell for any sympathy he can get, an' begins to push the straw back into his mouth. Then I says, "But all the same, it's not hurtin' as much when you pee, an' the dribblin' has slowed down a lot, eh?"

He nods again. "Yeh, it's better than it was . . ."

It takes Mark about a minute to realize his bell-captain is curin' a bad case of clap on the job. When he gets this to register in his small mind, he also thinks he's got to take action because there's three well-dressed people comin' through the door to register for rooms.

"Keep your hands out of the ice when preparin' ice buckets for customers," he tells his bell-captain. "Use ice-tongs!"

Those three gangsters barred me out of here for six months at one time. I'd run up a bill for seven or eight hundred, an' Matt was tryin' different ways of collectin' it. At first they were threatening, hinting my luggage could be seized an' the lock changed on my door. I laughed at them, sayin' if they was to do that, I'd consider my account settled with a plastic suitcase an' twenty dollars worth of socks an' underwear. So another time, Mark phones my room, coverin' the telephone mouthpiece with a handkerchief an' sayin' he was a collection agency. If I don't pay, they'll put me in jail, he says. I came down those stairs over there roarin'. When I get up to this desk, I take the edge of this tabletop an' tear out a four-foot strip of oak shelving, which I throw after Mark as he ducks out the side door.

I don't mind them tryin' to collect from me, it's their hotel. But show me some quality of thought, even in a den of fools. I despise dumb, cheap threats like "you pay me, or I'll burn your house down!"

They intercepted mail comin' to me, lookin' for cheques. My mail always got to me, but I knew it'd been handled over electric lights because of finger smudges on the envelopes. Matt never washes his hands. No cheques came, an' after two weeks of this Dick Tracy lark, they gave up.

I always pay my debts, kid. But for the first time in my life, them hoods began to bother me. I started wonderin' just what did I really owe them. You seen for yourself the hotel rooms I get — the worst rooms in the house for Romeo Kuchmir, because when he's in place it's home to him, an' he stays for six months. Okay, so I get a twenty percent discount, but twenty percent of what? What's my room worth when it's a hundred percent? The plaster's peelin', windows haven't been washed since the war ended, waterpipes play like an organ when I turn a tap to brush my teeth. I hear the languages of half the world through the walls, floor an' ceiling. An' when I need to crap, it's a half-mile walk down the corridor to the men's john, which is occupied half the times I need it.

Listen — the old punk who was night clerk before you walked through the buildin' every hour, lookin' for fires, an' free tail an' booze for himself. One night I'm waitin' at the door of the crapper, been waitin' like that for twenty minutes. Sam comes around the bend in the hallway, makin' his rounds.

"Sam," I says, "open this door with your passkey."

"There's someone in there. I can't do that. It's against regulations."

He was big on regulations, having served in the army. There's men who spend a few years in the army an' if they're lucky not to get themselves killed, go back home an' do useful things. There's another kind of man who learns to read regulations in the army. He spends the rest of his life polishin' his shoes an' bein' a cop to a garbage dump or a stack of two-by-four lumber joists. It's against regulations to piss in the sink. A broad who smokes in the airport will set a plane on fire. Beat the boy who pulls his wire . . .

"It's against hotel regulations, Romeo. I won't open the door."

"Don't make me mad, Sam. I can kick the feet out from under you an' take your keys an' your false teeth away from you. So you open this door, or I'm gonna rough you up!" Sayin' that, I give him a slight shove, enough to make him hit the corridor wall with his shoulder an' the back of his head. Right away I saw in his eyes that he was about to bend one regulation a bit. He took the passkey out of his pocket an' handed it to me.

"If anyone asks me, I'll say you forced me," he whines an' starts walkin' away. But I catch his arm an' pull him back.

"Hey, I want you to see this," I says to him.

I've got this one face you see, but in my profession I've learned to work it for myself like a hundred masks. I'm a good actor. I can cry, fake laughter, pain — anything. If your father died an' you had to work the day of his funeral, for ten dollars I could go an' cry for you. For you, for everybody in the family, two hours of solid cryin' of such a quality as to make people remember it five years after they'd buried him.

So, as I unlocked the door of the john, I twisted up my face to resemble that of a dinosaur with indigestion. Kickin' the door open so it hit the side wall with a wallop, I stepped into the doorframe, breathin' in deep an' spreadin' my elbows so I looked half again as big as I really am.

An' sittin' on the pot in that washroom was a consti-pated little barley farmer from Lac La Biche . . . peaked cap on his head, eyes waterin' with bowel strain . . . a day's growth of grey bristle on his face.

Good actin', kid, is a matter of power an' timing. When you come in like gang-busters, save on the sounds until all the other terror has sunk in. Then you let go. I bared my teeth an' growled before I moved to stand over him.

"Shit!" I commanded in the biggest voice I got. "You've been here twenty minutes — now shit!"

He did. What Exlax couldn't touch, fear drove through him like a blast from an air compressor. He was out of there in thirty seconds, empty an' white faced. I patted him on the back as he went out the door, bucklin' his pants. But when I did that, he yelped like he'd been touched by a brandin' iron.

It says in the bible the meek shall inherit the earth. I don't believe it, kid. All the meek will inherit is bad breath an' a hollow wind aroun' the heart.

I've been down an' out on my luck. But I've never begged, an' what I've borrowed, I've repaid with interest. When the wrestling game got slow, I used to be in business sellin' sacks of cement to gangsters who build houses for the poor in this country. I never had a warehouse or an office. Yet they always knew when I had surplus cement stacked up in some farmer's field with a plastic sheet over it.

Where did it come from, you ask? It was stolen. Not by me — by others. It was stolen from construction projects an' city supply sheds, but mostly from the government. You see, the way the system works, government buildings are supposed to be built to last. The same's bank buildings. Politically, it has to be that way. Wouldn't look good to have a government building fall under four feet of snow while the bank stands. Why vote for a government then? Go vote for a bank. There was a sayin' in my town that all roads in the world ended up at a gravel pile owned by a government minister . . . or his wife . . . or his brother. The gravel was there to build other roads to other gravel piles, but that's another story.

The smart contractor assures the government he's buildin' better. Oh, it'll cost a bit more, but it'll be a better building. For every two bags of cement, he'll see a third one gets put in the mixer. So he gets the contract. What goes into the buildin' after that is somethin' else. Cement disappears, carpets grow wings, government bought panelling ends up on the walls of the best homes in the west end.

So I buy cement from one crook for a dollar a bag an' resell it to another for a dollar-fifty. I only deal when I'm hard up, so I can't afford a warehouse. God provides me with an open field somewhere, an' from Woodwards I get a hundred yards of plastic sheet for ten bucks to cover my loot an' I'm in business for myself!

When I make a sale, the guy who buys sends a trucker to collect the load. The truckers they send are bums. They've got all kinds of reasons why they can't load cement bags by hand. So I usually end up loadin' it myself, or gettin' some kid to help for ten bucks an' a steak dinner in town when the job's done. But the money's good, an' I always come out ahead of the game.

The worst trucker I met in my business looked like one of them kodiak bears. Big shoulders, yellow fangs for teeth, an' hairy all over. You couldn't see the skin on his hands or fingers for this black hair. An' on his head it come down to meet his eyebrows. Neanderthal . . . the kind of animal who'd eat a suitcase if it contained raw meat.

"Hey, sport — how about helpin' out," I says to him after I'd carried four sacks into the truck, an' he's still hangin' around, kicking the tires on the back wheels of his truck.

"Can't."

"Why not?"

"I'm a sick man. I should be in bed. I'll die if I lift anythin'."

"What's hurtin'?"

"I'm sittin' on a Volkswagen inner tube to drive here — did you know that?"

"No, I didn't."

"I should be in hospital. I'm that sick. Or sittin' home in a hot bath."

He was beginning to bitch me off.

"What the hell's wrong with you? If you're a cripple then why come here? I need a healthy man to load this stuff!"

He looked up at me out of the bluest piggy eyes I ever seen in a dark hairy face. Christ, he was ugly.

"Well sir, I went to the store on Thursday an' bought me a pineapple. I had a cravin' for pineapple on Thursday. Would've done better if I'd bought a can of juice an' drunk that instead. But I cut the pineapple in two an' ate half of it. Never do that again . . ."

Right then I knew he wasn't as dumb as I thought he was. That he was spreadin' a good layer of bull under me, around me, an' over me. That he'd already spread it an' I was standin' in the middle in it up to my ankles.

"I've eaten a whole pineapple on a hot day. It's good for you. Lots of vitamins in a pineapple," he continues. Then he spits on the endgate where I'm standin'. He thinks for a moment, an' then goes on. "But not on a *cold* day. Never eat pineapple on a cold day. I ate half that pineapple an' within an hour, it blew my arsehole out!"

He had me. I made one desperate attempt to stop him.

"Friend, I've never met you before, " I says to him.
"I don't know your name or where you come from. You're
a stranger to me. I don't want to know you. I'm not in-
terested in your asshole. My religion don't allow that. I
don't wanna hear about it."

But that bastard wasn't listenin' to me.

"I came outa there on my hands an' knees. First guy I
seen was the shop foreman. "Get me a Volkswagen inner
tube an' blow it up!" I yell at him. The same inner tube I
got here in the truck with me now. "Put it in a car for me
to sit on, an' drive me to hospital," I holler at him again.

He cleared his throat an' spat at the endgate again.

"Well, sir, they got me in alright, an' two doctors worked
for an hour scrapin', cuttin' away the damages an' then
sewin' my blow hole back together again. I was sicker'n a
dog for weeks after. Had to learn to crap standin' up,
careful not to poop on my pantlegs like a baby."

"I don't want to hear about it — piss off! Get your
goddamned truck out of here — G'wan!" I wasn't shoutin'
at him so much as pleadin', but it was like askin' a locomotive the time of day.

"A guy like you takes his arsehole for granted. You
abuse it, sand it down with toilet paper, sit on ice or dive
into water feet first, an' legs apart. You wouldn't do that
if you'd a woman's equipment! You wouldn't do that to
your nostril, would you? They're both the same, you know.
You blow shit an' air outa both of them!"

"Okay, okay — when I next put Vicks up my nose I'll
do the same for my ass to keep it from feelin' bad, you
sonofabitch!" I says to him. "They got you all fixed up,
so give me a hand with the cement. What you know won't
make you a senator or a school teacher, but it shouldn't
stop you carryin' cement like other men!"

The last thing he had in mind was helpin' me.

"I'll never be the man I was, no sir. I should be walkin'
with a stick up the long hill to my death now. But I'm a

poor man, got to keep drivin' this fuckin' truck," he says. "A month after I come out of hospital I'm walkin' down a city street, bent over, me legs so wide apart a kid on a trike could drive through them. An old lady comes up behind me, walkin' stick in her hands, her knees thick as footballs with arthritis, her back humped over, mouth all shrivelled up, she's maybe a hundred an' ten years old. But she passes me goin' uphill like I was standin' still! How do you think that made me feel, eh? How do you think I felt? Go load cement yourself. I'm gonna rest in the cab. When you've loaded up, knock three times on the endgate so I'll know when to go."

Like you were tellin' me yesterday, kid — with computors an' new machines, life gets easier for the workin' man. I think it's good it's gettin' that way. I don't want my kids livin' like I lived. But what's gonna happen to guys like that trucker? If he gets an asshole pension, who's he goin' to fight? What purpose will his life have?

What's it goin' to be like for the rest of us, when we're left with no stories to tell? I read somewhere in a book that there's no sorrow in the just society. If there's no sorrow, where's the joy comin' from? I can't imagine anythin' more sad than a world where there's no sorrow. Because there'll be no room in such a world for a punk like that trucker.

four

You can teach dogs to listen, an' magpies to speak.

When I was a kid, my uncle Vladimir had a Saint Bernard dog whose name was Valentine Number Two. The name was too long to say if you were callin' him in a hurry. So instead he was called "boy". He was a big, stupid dog. With eye pouches too big for his eyes, lips too big for his mouth. He drank the toilet bowl dry at my uncle's house. He slept a lot in the shade of a poplar tree which grows in my uncle's front yard. Car rides excited "boy", an' when he was excited, he kept breakin' wind.

My uncle Vladimir drove his Chevrolet sedan with all windows open, winter an' summer, an' "boy" on the front seat beside him. Even so, for an hour after my uncle came home from a car trip with the dog, the car an' my uncle both smelled of dog fart.

When "boy" slept an' I wanted him to be up on his feet an' goin', all I had to say was, "Go, boy — go!"

"Boy" would be awake an' on his feet like he'd been spring loaded . . . tearin' up gravel an' runnin' this way an' that, growling, his eyes wild in their watery pouches tryin' to find what it was he was expected to chase.

"Go, boy — go!" I'd call an' point. He'd see the way I was pointin' an' go like hell in that direction until he'd hit a board fence. Then he'd reverse directions an' run like hell the other way, his rear end poppin' like bursts of rocket fire!

"Go, boy — go!"

An' he's off, woofin' an' snortin', over-turning buckets of water, garden rakes, upsettin' wheelbarrows an' rocking chairs until my uncle would catch him by the collar an' rassle his dumb dog to the ground.

"What the hell's the matter with you anyway?" he'd say an' pat "boy" on the head until he cooled off. Pretty soon he'd go to sleep, his big lips spread out like a puddin' around his mouth. The top of his eyes shut, but the bottom eye pouches extended like two meaty shoehorns.

I'd creep up behind the trees, an' makin' sure my uncle wasn't around to see me, would cough softly. Just like that, the stupid dog's eyes opened an' the head comes up, the curtain of lips followin', drooling saliva like a fishnet.

"Go . . ."

An' the dog's rear end is up, back paws dug into the ground.

"Leave boy alone, you goddamned bastard!"

My uncle Vladimir was in a corner of his garden where I hadn't expected him to be. He came towards me, his eyes hangin' from the tops of his sockets, his lips loose. He looked like "boy". I climbed the fence just ahead of a handful of pebbles he threw at me.

The followin' spring, I found a baby magpie that'd been chewed up by a cat. I kept him in a paper box an' fed him cornmeal, bits of hamburger an' milk. I began teachin' him to speak. You don't have to split a magpie's tongue to understand words he learns, that's not true. He won't learn many words. Even if he had a mouthful of tongue, he'd never learn the lord's prayer, but there's some things you can teach a magpie, split tongue or not.

When he was strong enough to fly, I let him out of the paper box. When I went for a walk, he'd fly to one side of me, then the other. Sometimes he'd fly ahead an' wait in a tree until I caught up to him.

"Go, boy — go!" he was shoutin' in a funny kind of voice, like you sometimes hear on an old recording. One day we're on a walk, an' approachin' my uncle's house. My uncle's gone to work in the lumberyard, his car's gone. An' "boy" is sleepin' on the sidewalk, beside the garden gate. The magpie flies ahead, glidin' past the dog an' settlin' on a picket of the fence. He kind of caws once an' flutters his wings. "Boy" lifts his head, looks up at the bird with one eye an' rolls over for more sleep.

"Go, boy — go!"

The stupid dog's feet was awake before the rest of him. They dig into the ground an' he's off down the street. The magpie tips his head, watchin' him go, then flies after him.

"Go, boy — go!"

"Woof! Woof!"

The dog's in high gear now, layin' down a cloud of dust mixed with the stench of dog fart behind him. A kid comin' around the corner on his bike is sent flyin' into a hedge. An' Missus Donnel's low-slung clothesline full of wet washing goes "plunk" as "boy" takes a shortcut through her yard an' clothesline into the next street.

That was the last I seen of either "boy" or my magpie. If they found enough to eat, they're probably to the bottom of South America now, for they were headin' that way when they left town. I felt it was like kind of a marriage. Each found what the other was lookin' for. An' because I was a kid then an' had time on my hands, I accidentally turned out to be a kind of marriage broker between them . . .

Marriage . . .

I've been married myself, kid. Had one baby — a boy. He's a teenager now. He's not like me — not at all. He wears thick glasses an' turtleneck sweaters. He wears sandals all summer an' needs a haircut. He doesn't live, he sits an' reads these big books on how wars were fought. It makes me laugh, seein' this half-blind little bugger readin' about how to kill! An' it's my kid, my seed made that one, that's for sure. Although there's a helluva lot of his mother there too. She had big, flat feet, same's him. An' a habit of rubbin' her left eye when she was worried. She rubbed that eye a lot when we were together.

When I'm worried, I laugh. I'm laughin' in the wrestlin' ring. I laugh when a letter from the bank tells me I'm poorer now than I was the day I was born. I'll tell you somethin' else, kid —I'll be laughin' the day I die!

I laugh at what the heart an' wang of a man takes him to when he's lonely — a woman. Especially a *good* woman. Nancy was one of them — a *good* woman. What a helluva thing to say about a broad! They're condemned before they're tried. Who cares if a man tells his friends he married a good woman.

"Hey, guys — I got married!"

"Yeh? Who'd you marry?"

"A broad called Janet, but that don't matter. She's a whore an' a shoplifter!"

In five minutes, every guy in the plant is pumpin' your hand, askin' you to a party, slappin' your shoulder. You're somebody, an' so's your Janet! The world's too full of good people. We need bastards now to liven things up, or we'll sink in a puddle of goodness.

We were nothin' when we married, Nancy an' me. But hand in hand, from spoon to mouth, as they say, we first collected a rockpile an' then built a house. An' after that, the start of a life. Nothin' of value comes easy. Not a marriage. Not a child. Not even knowin' what's inside of you.

We began as muck, along with the mosquitos an' lice. The bugs went their way, doin' what bugs do. But someone put his lips to our earhole an' whispered somethin' about god, about becomin' god ourselves. An' we're just stubborn an' tough enough not to forget that. But it's no four-lane highway gettin' there, believe me.

You know what eats up a man from the inside out? It's the curse of withholdin'. No man trusts another. Leave two men in a room for ten minutes an' you've got two liars layin' down bullshit.

"I killed the biggest moose in the world two years ago, up by Fort Saint John!"

"Oh, yeh? But I've got the thickest cock on the prairies!"

Never do they say — "Brother, help me. I'm small an' mean an' I don't know what I'm doin', can you help me?"

Women are different. They tell each other everythin'. They trust each other, even when they're enemies. They hate an' love an' call to each other for help. An' each one gives love an' support to the other. They withhold nothin'. I've been told there's cases where the wife of a man, an' another woman he's been screwin' on the side, they'll meet, an' talk, an' cry while holdin' on to each other like sisters. Now if that's true, an' I don't know if it is, but if that's true, then it's special! That's two hills an' a mountain above us. It tells *me*, a punk who's never learned to speak one language well enough to be understood, that women are up there. Near enough to get the almighty by his ankle an' ask him — "See this, boss? Is it good enough? Is this what you wanted?"

Not so with men. They're afraid to confide an' cry an' kiss an' hold each other. A friend of mine, a Greek wrestler who reads books, an' who liked to eat hot sauerkraut an' stewed rabbit, he once told me he read somewhere that Greek soldiers in a war used to put down their guns at night an' meet the enemy soldiers to share food an' a place to sleep. In the morning, they separated to shoot at each other all day, because two kings far away said they had to. That's not the same thing as with the women. That's not love. It's despair.

Why do you look at me that way, kid? There's somethin' in your eyes that's afraid. Is it because I tell you I love men that makes you afraid? I love women, an' when I tell you about that, you smile. But with men . . .

Kid, I could make a faggot out of you in an hour if I put my mind to it. An' you'd do it to the next guy you liked, so don't look at me that way. I'm a lover, not a killer. What my hands or lips touch gives life, not death.

If you were dyin', an' all the medicines couldn't help you, all that would save you was to be held or touched a certain way, count on me to help you. That's all I have to say! But let me ask you somethin', would you do the same for me? Would you ever forgive me if you did?

You can't answer me, can you? The disease is already inside of you, workin' away.

I'm sad about many things. I would like to wear rings on my hands, an' shirts with puffy sleeves, an' more gold in my teeth. An' expensive perfume . . . the kind that makes people stop, turn an' smile when I'm walkin' through. Shoes of red leather like they use to bind old books. Then everybody'd notice me, eh? Then they'd say — "Hey, there goes a *man*!"

I want what I can't have. A rose behind my ear an' sexy oil on my skin. I hate Taiwan underarm perspirant an' one-way sunglasses — that's for pimps an' watch thieves. I'm a man from where the pine trees grow, an' the wind burns like it's comin' from the smokestacks of hell! That's the way I am, an' that's the way I love. No holds barred, nothin' but the best, even if I know I'll never get it!

It's not my fault if I scare you talkin' like this. It's two o'clock in the morning. The hour men die in their sleep, or think of death if they're awake. There are things which make me sad. I'm a wrestler. I could've sung opera, or been the captain of a ship.

My life wasn't much. But it's better than some lives I've known.

There was a guy called Shwartz, disabled an' on pension. He married Nina Bergman, who preached each summer just outside our town. Shwartz was thin an' tall, walkin' with a limp an' one arm frozen by his side.

Nina was a young, willowy broad with big, dark eyes an' a smile that'd turn your mind if you were a guy, any guy. But especially if you were a young punk wantin' real bad to see up a woman's skirt for the first time. Yeh, Nina had every young hood in town turnin' over an' sweatin' himself sick tryin' to fall asleep at night.

Maybe it was the age we were, an' seein' things different. She had this pubic hump showin' even when she wore a skirt an' stood up straight. The broad was made for screwin', not bible-thumpin' an' living with a crippled man at least thirty years older than herself. She was *juicy*, an' so were we. Anyhow, she played the accordion, sang hymns an' preached. The services were held in an old school about four miles out of town. Shwartz an' she rented the school each summer, as well as the teacherage, where they lived. A week before the preachin' started, she had posters all over town . . . big posters, with her standin' life-size, opening her accordian, an' always that damned smile that got you so. Somewhere in the background of the poster, a bible under his arm an' a lost prairie farmer look on his face, was Shwartz. Them were good posters. I use her ideas today in my wrestlin' promotions.

About a week after she was in business, there'd come a night when a bunch of young punks an' myself from town decided to attend her revival meeting. She'd been botherin' our dreams from the previous summer, an' it was something of a pilgrimage we had to make — a rites of puberty sort of thing. We went down in the truck I drove part-time for the feed mill that year.

There was more to it than just Nina. It was the time of year . . . the heat of the summer, the broads around town wearin' less an' less. Fresh summer food an' the boredom of growin' up with nothin' to do. The pressure startin' building up, an' nobody less than Nina could relieve us. She knew it — I know now she knew it — an' that promising little lump of hers pulled us in like becs to honey. We needed tail so bad we ached all over. She gave us the word of god instead!

I'll tell you this, kid: in the heat of the summer, when

you're a young punk with the bud breakin' open, that rounded little hump of hers had more pull than a CPR locomotive, an' that's no lie!

So we went down, the guys all in the back of the truck, their shirt fronts open to catch the evening wind on their bodies. When we got there, the service had started. Nina was playin' her accordion at the front of the classroom, her body swayin' in a bright green dress which showed everythin' we came to see. Behind her was Shwartz, in baggy pants an' a grey shirt three sizes too large around the neck. Right up front were the young broads, an' behind them sat some old men an' women, bent over their prayerbooks like death at a picnic. We walked in an' took what seats were left at the back of the room. The young broads could smell us comin' in. They looked at us, got red-faced, giggled and turned away, because there were flames burnin' up our clothes an' rising to lick our faces an' damp hair.

"God is like a golden harvest," Nina was sayin' in her soft, breathless little voice. "God is like a summer rain, cooling our bodies, sweeping goodness an' love through winds of piety an' faith. Believe in god as I do, an' we shall all walk hand in hand down the footpaths of salvation!"

She smiled a goddamned sexual floodlight, her eyes an' mouth washin' over us like the wind of paradise. The guys around me were starin' straight ahead, their eyes glazed, mouths hangin' slack. Each one of those bastards was seein' himself hand in hand with Nina, walkin' down the road to salvation. But the road was twisted . . .

"The lord is my shepherd, I shall not want . . ."

It led up dark ladders into haymows . . . the back seats of cars parked in a woodlot . . . hot barley fields with the cunt-smell of sun an' summer earth . . .

"He leads me to green pastures . . ."

She picked up the accordion again, an' setting a beat with her hip an' foot, led the hymn singing. That goddamned red-pleated accordion flowered open an' shut in a regular kissin' motion that was makin' the punks around me start to cross their legs. Up front, the little broads in pigtails was singin' in loud voices. The punks an' myself in back sang in monotone, a sewin' machine chorus. The old timers between us couldn't follow the words fast enough, so they just stared at their books.

Then suddenly it all ends. Shwartz is at the door, his shoulders slouched an' his eyes watery like those of an old dog. He's handin' out chapters of scripture on cheap paper an' thankin' us for coming as we shuffle out the door. We walk past him, starin' past him, for *she's* out there at the bottom of the steps. She's not handin' out anything. She doesn't have to. Her smile's tired now, sweat tricklin' down her cheeks. We walk past her with our eyes down, a dull ache in the bottom of our stomachs spreadin' like a wound. Her voice is a dark whisper in the evening air.

"God bless you, brother . . . come again!"

The punks I came with all move to the truck. We're not sayin' anything. We lean against the side of the door an' hood an' pass cigarettes around. It's late evening now, the sky an' low spots on the ground gettin' dark. The people move away, some walking, some drivin'. We just stand there, watchin' Shwartz an' Nina go back into the school, then come out with their books. She's carryin' her accordion over her shoulder, like a rucksack.

They cross towards the teacherage, Nina in front an' the old man followin'. They don't once look over to where we're standin' beside the truck. They're talkin' . . . or rather, she's sayin' something, an' Shwartz just nods his head. A slight wind starts up, blowin' the sound of her voice to us. She's sore about somethin' . . .

"Well, you'll go tomorrow and you'll tell them to go screw themselves. I've got enough to worry about!"

We heard her say it — we heard her say it loud an' clear. An' yet, we didn't. She had us so tenderized from the prayer meetin' we didn't believe she would talk like we did.

To this day, I was there an' I know what she said, but I don't believe I heard it. It's like being told that Christ had bad breath, or my mother gettin' clap when she was seventeen. I never asked to know, an' if you tell me, I didn't hear you!

We kept lookin' after them until they reached the teacherage, an' she unlocked the door an' went in first. He followed, but she shut the door in his face as he was about to step in. He turned away, shrugged an' sat down on the step, his head buried in his hands.

It was gettin' dark now, but we continued lookin' where Shwartz sat until it got too dark to see him clearly anymore.

"Let's go," I says, an' opened the door of the truck.

"It's alright for you sittin' on a soft seat. We got to stand in back of the truck. I got to jack off first, or the bumpin' will kill me," says Bruno Prentice, a big kid with acne on his neck. Bruno worked for the house painter in town, an' his shoes were always spattered with paint.

"Me, too," says somebody from around the front of the truck, an' we all moved down the schoolyard towards the well, which was surrounded by a willow hedge.

We were laughin' now, shovin' against each other, shovin' with our shoulders an' our hips, prisoners of one woman, but marchin' away from her — goddamned revolutionaries, that's how we felt! The well was encased in spruce planks. A round chamber sunk into the ground, with a suspended pulley from which a bucket was hangin' somewhere down in the water. Most of the well was surrounded by this willow hedge nobody planted. It just growed there.

Bruno Prentice an' a punk named Pat Gorman who fixed bicycles in the Esso garage was hunched over in the middle of the clearin', talkin' in a whisper an' laughin. We heard them unzip themselves. The rest of us kind of stood around on one foot, scratchin' the back of our ankles with the toe of the other foot, hands in our pockets.

"Bet you a buck I can beat you to the draw an' shoot first!"

"Betcha can't!"

An' the match was on. We couldn't see too good, it was dark now, but we heard both of them breathin' hard.

"Here's for the holy ghost in your tight little ass, Nina!" I heard Bruno say in a thick, hoarse voice. About the same time I heard the well pulley creak behind where I stood. The bucket plopped back in the water, an' old Shwartz lit his flashlight. The light picked up Bruno, who was half-squattin' now in agony an' squirtin' a stream of sperm all over Pat Gorman's bare arms, an' there was Pat holdin' his own big stub in two hands an' pumpin' for the counter-attack.

The Gorman kid was the first to run, right through the willows, still holdin' on to himself. Those of us watchin' moved away from the light, leavin' Bruno Prentice alone in the light, his face and shirt wet with perspiration, his dink still skippin', but the look in his eyes scared now.

"What the hell you lookin' at?" he says in a thin, dry voice. "You got one of these, same's me, same's everybody!"

"Filthy, corrupt pigs! May god damn every one of you," the old man says, an' droppin' the empty bucket he carried, he shuffles away into the darkness . . .

She bothered our dreams a lot that winter an' the summer following. But we never went back to watch her sing an' preach. Why bother?

You can't catch rain with outstretched hands, so why try the impossible? Bruno Prentice took up with a young widow that year. The rest of us hung around my old man's poolhall rememberin' summer.

five

It's better to wrestle for a livin' than raise turkeys. You become famous wrestlin'. Who remembers a turkey farmer?

I *eat* turkeys, tear them apart an' eat them, an' with the strength I get from the meat, I wrestle. Someplace there's a guy in a Hong Kong shirt, rubber boots an' straw hat carryin' buckets of turkey mash all day until his ass is draggin' on the ground, feedin' his turkeys so Romeo Kuchmir can wrestle. I think about that, an' I feel good! I feel good like a king feels good, or the superintendent of a parkin' lot: things keep movin' to keep me goin'!

A man's got to crow. That's what bein' a man is all about. To ride a horse, catch a fish, wrestle another man to the ground — that's the spice of it all. I like to drive, but I don't. Because when I drive a car, it's got to go a hundred miles an hour or I'm not livin'! Sure, you can kill somebody or yourself doin' that, but it's a better way to die than sittin' watchin' Bugs Bunny on television an' worryin' about your heart stopping . . . or feedin' fuckin' turkeys.

So when I promote a fight, I have posters made the size of blankets. In the middle of the poster is a life-size picture of me — Romeo Kuchmir, ex-wrestler, boxer an' promoter. All around me are small pictures of the fighters I promote. That's the way I see myself, an' I'm gonna share my vision with the world!

Sure, they give me static for that. But they got to bend or they're on the breadline. They give me static because after a match, I get the best booze an' the best screwin' for myself. The others get beer an' clap. I deserve it, kid — nothin' wrong with that. I'm an enterpriser, a capitalist

61

with forty cents in my pockets. I'm not equal to some oxhead with a thick neck who counts on his fingers! No two men are born equal. They never was an' they never will be.

So under this system, I use what I was born with. That's why I eat turkeys someone else grows for me, an' I feel good about it.

I've got nothin' against communism. If it keeps children from starvin', that's reason enough for me to believe in it. But don't fool yourself, kid — the same kind of people rise to the top. Khruschev wore pants which hung down at the butt an' on his head he had a sheepskin cap, the super workin' man! In America he would've wore a grey suit, an' made it as president of General Motors.

A frightened man, useless in the head, will always remain frightened an' useless in the head. Don't knock on the door — kick it open if you're comin' through. An' don't talk to secretaries. Secretaries are there to talk to other secretaries. The same with clerks an' painters in the hall. Go straight to the king an' ask for money!

There's a restaurant down the street called "The Flamingo". I go there one night last winter for a feed of liver an' onions. The waitresses there know me good . . . nice little broads who like to laugh a lot.

As I'm goin' in, I stick a set of these Dracula teeth into my mouth. Got them for two bits at a novelty store. Used to be a time when they sold things like pocket knives with mother of pearl inlay, key rings, cheap jewellery which looked expensive for two days until the shellac wore off. Now the novelty stores sell you plastic monster teeth, rubber cocks for a well-hung stallion, spiders the size of a baseball mitt with red eyes. What's happened to the class, an' the special kind of magic they once had?

I stick these teeth into my mouth, screw up my face an' make my eyes look dead. I drop one shoulder, blow out my stomach, make my feet drag like they was made of cement. I come through the door of "The Flamingo" an' sit at the counter. Patsy, the red-haired waitress with green eyes is leanin' on the counter across from me, readin' about Elizabeth Taylor in a magazine.

"Yes," she says, still readin'.

"I'm lookin' for the girl who made me sick," I says in a thick voice.

"This isn't a hospital," she replies without lookin' up. "This is a restaurant. Do you want coffee?"

"Yah . . . They said to come here for the business. I don't see no business. They got a business room in the back, maybe?"

She looks up at me now, an' jumps back against the wall. The Elizabeth Taylor magazine falls on the floor. I grin. She puts her hands over her mouth, an' then she knows who I am an' turns red in the face.

"Jesus Christ," she says, "that's an awful thing to do when it's not expected. Stop doin' that, Romeo. There's some cops having supper in the booth. If they see you lookin' like that, they'll pull you in."

"Send a message to them. Tell them they stink, tell them there's a man waitin' who's set fire to their car," I said an' grinned again. She looked away when I did that. A couple of seats down the counter, there's this drunk who interrupts our conversation.

"Hey, red," he hollers. "I ordered a steak! Where's my goddamn steak, lady?"

Patsy leaves me an' goes to the kitchen. She comes back with his steak plate, which she puts down in front of him. Then she goes to the urn to get him a coffee. The drunk pokes at the steak with his fork an' knife. Then he looks at Patsy, whose back is turned to us as she's pourin' coffee. That old bastard takes the steak in his hand an' before I realize what he's up to, he half-rises an' heaves it at her. It misses that little broad's head by an inch, hits the coffee machine an' falls on the floor.

"Goddamn meat ain't cooked right!" the drunk swears, his chin out, nostrils twitchin'.

No university psychologist will ever know what a broad who's five-foot-three an' works in a restaurant at night has to know to survive. This one's cool . . . super cool, as she carries the coffee to the drunk. She puts it in front of him, then goes back to the coffee machine. She picks up the steak in her hand, carries it back to where he's half-standin', an' slams it hard on his plate. The potatoes an' carrots on the plate fly into the old bastard's lap an' slide down the front of his pants.

"Eat!" she says. "Or your fuckin' head comes off!"

"Sure, red . . . sure. No need to get sore. I was only funnin' . . ."

He's beat. She's half his size, but he's not gonna move until she tells him to. The cops who've eaten in back of the restaurant are comin' out now. They pay Patsy.

"You should see a dentist," one of them says to me. Cops' jokes are the kind you remembered an' forgot when you were twelve.

"Your mother said that too. She was gonna break windows, so I paid a cab to take her home," I says. They look me up an' down, all three of them, an' decide it'd cost them more bruises than it was worth to extract an apology. So instead they all go "ha-ha-ha" an' leave. The drunk finishes his food, pays an' starts to stagger for the door. I wink at Patsy, an' she grins back at me.

"How . . . how . . . how . . . how!" I'm barkin' at the old bastard an' followin' him out.

We're on the street. It's colder now. A frozen wind, full of ice particles, has started blowin' from the north. The drunk turns to me, grinnin'.

"You're sure not pretty, you're fuckin' ugly," he says to me, an' offers his hand for a handshake. I grab it an' bite his wrist. He's goin' like hell down the sidewalk now, weavin' from side to side. I'm after him, right behind him, pickin' up speed, barkin' like hell. He turns into a doorway an' faces me. I can see he's scared now, still drunk but scared.

"A joke's a joke, buddy! Now piss off. I'm an old man an' I've been drinkin' pretty good, but I can still take care of myself!"

I'm fillin' up the doorway, growlin', my arms out like a gorilla. I roll up my eyes until only the whites are showin'. He ducks under my elbow an' is runnin' up the street.

"How! How! How!"

The snowplows have been through, leavin' piles of ice here an' there off the edge of the street. He picks up a lump of ice an' turnin' quickly, throws it at me.

"Urrr!" I flex my chest muscles an' the lump of ice bounces back.

"Goddamn sonofabitch! You're crazy!" He's shoutin' as he runs out into the street to flag a taxi that's approachin'. I'm right behind him, also wavin' my arms. The guy drivin' the cab is Lennie, the bootlegger. Lennie knows right away I'm doin' my bit for A.A., an' throwin' the back door open, he gives me a little wink. The drunk jumps in. I'm right behind him, even though he tries to yank the door shut between himself an' me.

"Where to?" asks Lennie.

"Fourth . . . down the hill!" the drunk squeals.

"How! How! Grr!" That's me. The drunk is sober now, an' pressed into a round lump against the cab door.

"Hey!" He changes his mind. "Drive to the police station!"

Lennie doesn't hear him. I lurch for the old fellow, an' he's climbin' up against the rear window of the car. I grab his leg an' bring the plastic teeth hard into his ankle. He screams out a kind of sound you don't expect to hear from any man — old or young — this side of hell. A kind of high bleat, like from a small animal standin' on four feet.

Lennie drives down to Fourth on the flats. It's only about two blocks of avenue there, snugged back in from the powerhouse. The old bastard throws a ten dollar bill at Lennie an' bolts out the door, runnin' for a square little house with a big front window.

"Drive around the block an' meet me back here in a minute, before the fuzz does," I tell Lennie, an' go after the drunk. He's through the front door before I get there, an' I hear the lock turn inside. The lights go on. I'm barkin' loud now an' go to the window. The lights in surrounding houses are comin' on. Inside the livingroom, the drunk is yellin' something up the stairs. Pretty soon I see a pissed-off old lady with curlers in her hair an' a cheap dressin' gown around her body comin' down the stairs. She's flat-footed an' walks painfully.

I'm scratchin' at the window an' poundin' the glass, growlin', the plastic teeth bared. He's pointin' at me, an' as she looks to where he's pointin', I press my face hard against the window. I can imagine what it looks like from the other side, an' I'm right. One look at me an' she's goin' right back upstairs. The dressin' gown falls off her an' the last I seen of her, she's runnin', her bare ass bouncing, runnin' with her hands an' feet to get the hell out of there. I grin at the prick an' wag my finger for him to come to me. He backs towards the fireplace. He's scared . . . *really* scared now.

There's a glass swan on the mantelpiece beside him. He's lookin' around, his eyes rollin' wildly, sees the swan, an' grabbin' it, he throws it at me. The window is a double sash winter window. The glass swan comes through the first glass but not the second. By now I figure he's ready to flip an' end up in a bird cage. Besides, Lennie's cab has pulled up to the sidewalk behind me. So with a last, lone-wolf howl, I back away, stampin' my feet like I'm fightin'' against some invisible dog leash from inside the taxi.

Lennie drives back to "The Flamingo" an' we have hot coffee an' a few laughs with Patsy. Then we go to Lennie's place an' kill a bottle of scotch for which I pay twelve dollars. Patsy has two drinks an' wants to play, but I'm old enough to be her father, an' the worries of the world sit on my head like a sack of sand. I can't help her. Lennie's gone to drive his cab. We're in his apartment, she's sittin' on my knee an' gettin' sore because I'm starin' out the window, sad as an orphan boy.

"You bastard," she says to me. "What's wrong? Has there been another woman?"

"You ever seen flood or drought?" I ask her. "Do you know how deep a man can hurt for other men?"

She's off my knee an' in the kitchen, pourin' black coffee for herself, her face hard as stone.

"Listen to me," I say to her. "What a man an' a woman do when they're connected in the middle is a celebration. But you've got to hurt so you deserve to celebrate. We grow older, we see the years go by in the house we've built, the children we had grow into men an' women themselves."

"Piss off," she says, swallowin' hot coffee like she was dyin' of thirst.

"I'm hurtin' for the man who spends all his life, workin' at a job he hates, payin' for a home that rots away faster than he pays for it. Yet he'll work harder than if he was a slave, because in the north, winter is the enemy. Winter is like death sittin' in a corner, waitin'. But we laugh at death, by laughin' at ourselves!"

"What concern is that to me?" she asks, the cup in her small hands shakin'. "I've got a good job an' a place to live. On Saturday night, I go dancin'."

"So dance," I says to her. "Dance until your feet hurt an' your skin glows like stars in the night. That's what bein' young is all about. Dance an' holler. That black sonofabitch winter is scared of that. Have a good meal when you're hungry, an' a good lay with a man your equal when you're lonely. But remember, that's a celebration an' an 'up yours' to winter, an' the men of winter."

"What men of winter?" She looks at me with tears in her eyes.

"The men I understand an' envy, but whom I'll never join because broads like you are eatin' out my heart. The lenders an' collectors who never lift a board or mix a bucket of cement, who go to church, send their kids to college on your back."

Patsy's laughin' now an' throws her cup into the sink where it breaks into a hundred pieces.

"Jesus Christ, Romeo, I thought for a while you were sick!" she says.

"An' when that man's dyin', the newspapers show his picture an' cry. An' you, dumb, law-abidin' tit, cry with them. You cry more than his widow, because you're warm an' healthy." I get it all out an' I'm weak. She's back on my knee, stroking my hair back here behind the ears.

"I'd cry for you if you died, Romeo," she says. "I'd cry for you one year without stoppin'. Because I'm soft-hearted like my mother. She cried all day when she heard the king of England died."

Me, I don't cry for anyone, kid. To cry is to forgive. I get so sad I can't catch my breath sometimes, but I'll never forgive. So I'm an enterpriser, a freewheelin' bandit who follows the big bully an' picks up scraps of what's left without bendin' a knee to get it. I'll never work for another man, an' I'll never work for wages. There's people who call me nothin' but a well-dressed bum. I owe to hotels an' restaurants, but nobody burns me for that, or I'll drive a size-ten boot up their ass!

I've been kicked out of this hotel. Told never to come back. Six months later, I'm promotin' a big fight here. A contender for the world heavyweight title has come in for a share of the gate, as well as four wrestlers famous from here to Mexico City. Good advance ticket sales. I come through that door askin' for a room. The same guys who threw me out now carry my suitcases upstairs. One afternoon, I'm carryin' twenty grand in this pocket, an' it feels like a nice, warm twat.

I show them the roll, an' they're touchin' it like it was the Virgin Mary's facecloth. Matt is sniffin' at it. Clapper has tears in his eyes he's so impressed.

I can make telephone calls to New York, papers are carryin' my ads. The clerks an' bellhops are bringin' up enough free sandwiches an' coffee to feed all the bums on skid row. The biggest businessmen in town are comin' through my door like I was a one-man massage parlor. They're offerin' to invest money, time. For two weeks the whole world knows me by first name.

"Hello, Romeo. How ya doin', boy?"

"How about a drink, Romeo, old cock? It's on me!"

"Hey, Romeo . . . Jesus, man, you haven't changed! You don't look a day older than when I seen you in the ring, when? Four, five years back?"

'Fifteen years ago, you prick!" I tell them. "I retired from liftin' anything heavier than my suitcase fifteen years ago!"

"Oh, yeh? Still the same old Romeo, heh, heh! You don't look a day older. How do you do it?"

"Snake liver . . . I eat snake livers for breakfast!"

"Come on, you've got a secret, but you're not tellin', is that it?"

They throw a dinner for me night before the match at the best restaurant in town. The mayor's there, so are the car dealers. I buy myself a white suit an' patent leather shoes. I get my hair washed in a beauty saloon an' dried with an electric dryer. I buy a bottle of good french cologne an' have a sponge bath in it. When I come through the front door of that restaurant, it's like Al Capone himself comin' to a christening. Every broad in the room smells me before she sees me. I come in like a stud, gold tooth gleamin' in the biggest smile I can stretch out, my eyes sparklin' like I was on a one-thousand percent make!

They bring out the best food I've ever eaten. They make speeches, talkin' about me. They talk about me puttin' the city on the map with such big names comin' over from the United States. They talk about culture for the common man, how the country is growin' up, that work, hard work, has its rewards. How enrichin' it is for the common man to have a chance to see a good fight.

While they're talkin, I'm eatin' an' drinkin' their cognac an' laughin'. I'm laughin' as I give a couple of good-lookin' broads the feel, right under the noses of their husbands, who don't know, because they're talkin' so they can make back the money they've invested. That's the best kind of feel, somethin' with conspiracy an' danger to it, kid. Put your dink near an open weasel trap an' see it come alive!

There's more cognac an' coffee, an' the speeches are comin' from other tables now. The chief of police promises support. Two guys from trade unions, who look like chiefs of police on their days off, promise to display my posters, because they know me an' are my friends.

I never seen them before.

There's other friends I don't know . . . guys standin' up an' tellin' stories about when an' how they knew me . . . where an' for how long. I'm addin' numbers in my head, an' pretty soon I figure I'm a hundred an' twenty years old to know them all the way they say. I get up an' thank them all for comin', an' say that I wished my mother was alive to see all the friends I had. I can't say anymore because I'm laughin', an' they're all laughin' because I'm laughin'. I leave.

Outside the door of the restaurant, I lean against the wall because I'm dizzy an' confused. A bull feels dizzy an' confused when he breaks a barbed wire fence an' knows there's nothin' holdin' him. One of the broads I'd felt under the table, the wife of an advertising executive, comes toward me. She winks an' asks if there's something I'd forgotten. I reach for my wallet, but it's there, an' seein' this, she laughs.

Arm in arm we walk across the street to the first hotel, check in under phoney names an' shack up until the sun comes in through the window next day. This one's a real pro, the one-timer who burns a blister on your brain. Whose little machine workin' overtime in the proper bedrooms can send a thousand fightin' men to keep peace in Cyprus the next day! She's everywhere; in the closet, against the wall, under an' over you. The kind you'd beat at her game the second time 'round, but not the first. Only tonight, she's doin' it for fun an' practice. Tomorrow she'll be usin' it to make promotions for her husband, or her friends, but not tonight!

She's still sleepin' in the morning when I leave her. I clip a fifty dollar bill into her hair, so she's sure to see it when she goes into the bathroom. Doin' that, I paint a line between them an' me.

Doin' that leaves me free. I'm a hustler who owns nothin', an' doin' that leaves me free to burn their house down.

SIX

six

I can't sleep at night. I haven't slept all night in years. I wake up at noon an' then I'm up until four next mornin'. What happens to a man when he does that?

I'm not alone. There's night people in every city — newspapermen, hustlers, bootleggers, pastry cooks, guys like you on night shift, cops, burglars, taxi drivers. Sometimes I feel like my skin's been washed by stars an' black wind. Then I hear a jet up in heaven, headin' for daylight an' Honolulu where it's warm, an' I feel good an' glad to be among the night people. Because among us there's guys with the power to leave it all an' take three hundred others with them!

In the basement, back of the hotel, there's a bakery. An old punk called Simon works there at night, mixin' up dough for butterhorns an' cinnamon buns which he's baked for breakfast in the restaurant by morning. Simon's not as old as he looks. But he's old. Worried old like a Jewish saint. His oldest boy is doin' eight years in the slammer for armed robbery. Simon lost his house last summer in a poker game. When the house went, so did his wife.

So Simon lives alone in a boardin' house where his bed an' breakfast cost him seventy a month. In two years he'll get old age pension, an' he'll sit in a window with a geranium pot an' look down at the street, thinkin'.

When I see a geranium pot, I kick the fuckin' thing against a wall. Did you know that you have to work at killing a geranium? Even after it's been tipped over an' the roots have dried in the sun, a Thursday missionary can set it back in the pot again an' the goddamned thing grows? I hate the smell of geraniums; they smell like laundry in a home for incurables. An' it's the flower that's put around old people to remind them they're gonna die soon. Give me lilacs an' roses. Fuck geraniums!

Simon works down in the basement. He comes to work an hour after you do. You seldom see him. He moves in the shadows, even at night. By two o'clock he's got the sweet dough mixed. An' while it's risin', he lays down on the flour board next to the oven an' goes to sleep.

Simon is a funny kind of sleeper. There's as many different kinds of sleepers as there's people. Some sleep curled up like babies, knees under their chins. For some, sleep's the last day of their lives — they fight, grind their teeth, groan an' plead. Simon needs heat when he sleeps, an' he gets heat from the oven. The room he works in is one big heat box. An' he's not too clean. The clothes he wears under his baker's apron are caked with dough an' stink of sweat an' yeast.

I don't know what he dreams about when he's sleepin', but whatever it is, it makes him reach for his crotch. If he dreams long enough, he'll get himself unbuttoned an' his hands around the throat of the northern kangaroo with two swollen legs.

He's got an alarm clock now. But before you came to work here, he had an arrangement with the guy who had your job. Sam was to wake Simon at four in the morning, so he'd get his pastry cut an' in the oven for the seven o'clock restaurant trade. One night, Sam gets a rush of late registrations, so he gives me the key an' sends me down to wake the baker.

I find the baker spread out on the flour board, his hair an' clothes all covered in flour. His legs are apart, his shoes are off. One sock is hangin' on by the toes, while the other looks like it's just been pulled on. An' Simon's hangin' on with both hands to the purple mother what's ready to whamo if you so much as touch it with a goose feather.

"Hey!" I poke him in the ribs. "Time to wake up."

He's up on his ass, bendin' from the hips like a robot. His eyes shut, his wang still at half-mast, he's on his feet an' headin' for the vat, which has a balloon top of warm dough. No time to wash his hands of his fantasies or crotch sweat, he's into the dough, flattenin' it down so's he can roll it out into flat slabs for cutting. Once he's punched the dough down, he's awake.

"Thanks, rassler," he says. "I must've dozed off. Don't tell anyone. I'm not in the habit of sleepin' on the job, so don't say anythin', eh?"

"Don't you ever wash your hands before doin' that?" I ask him. He looks at his hands then at me. He's puzzled.

"What for? They're clean."

I swallow somethin' that's come up into my throat to choke me an' turn to leave. He catches my sleeve.

"Hey," he says. "Sit down. I'm makin' some coffee. There's lots of leftover doughnuts, butterhorns, cinnamon buns. No sense payin' for them in the restuarant when I've got 'em here. Sit down."

"Screw you an' your butterhorns!" I said to him an' left.

I don't ask anyone how bread is made, or noodles, or morning hotcakes. I could starve to death if I asked.

A loaf of bread can get you into trouble. I once threw a loaf of bread out of my hotel room window. Three stories down. I aimed for an' hit a college kid in the kiester with it. I knew it was a college kid because he wore a suede leather jacket an' jeans. Only a kid with enough money for university can dress like that an' get away with it. An ordinary kid wears denim jackets with jeans.

Anyway, this punk was standin' around waitin' for a bus at eleven o'clock at night. What the hell's a kid his age doin' at a bus stop this late at night? I was feelin' low, had drunk up all my booze, didn't have money for a fresh bottle. The last twenty dollars I had I'd blown three hours ago takin' a broad with the monthlies to dinner at the steak house. She waited until she'd eaten before she told me her troubles. So what the hell. I buy this loaf of bread, just in case I can't swing breakfast in the morning.

It's summer, an' I'm sittin' at my window lookin' down an' I see this kid waitin' for his bus. I don't want breakfast, I think to myself — I want some action. So I take good aim an' fire the loaf down. It hits the kid in the mug. His little beanie flies off, an' he flips over. The loaf of bread's wrapped in plastic that's tougher than bomb casing, an' it's still in one piece. The kid picks it up, then himself, an' looks up at me. I give him a raspberry.

"Sir, did you throw this?" he asks me in the nice voice of a lawyer who's about to burn you.

"Damned right I did!", I holler down at him. "What's wrong? You want me to throw down some marmalade an' butter as well?"

"Sir, why did you throw it at me?"

Right then, somethin' inside me says — watch it. This isn't an ordinary kid goin' to college so's he can make more money. This is one of those I'll-wear-you-down-mothers who don't have to lift a hand to nail you in a corner. He'll tie you up with his mouth, providin' he's got an audience.

Just then, his audience was crossin' the street in size-twelve boots. A big, rawboned rookie of a cop with legs that start where other men have belly-buttons, an' a haircut so short his neck looks blue under it.

"You're a university punk . . . I know that! Go set a school on fire, do something' useful!" I'm brayin' down in a voice that's sayin', "I never read a book in my life an' I'm proud of it." He smirks up at me an' then turns to the cop.

"Sir," he calls the cop over. "The gentleman in the room up there threw this loaf of bread with great velocity at me, knocking off my hat an' spectacles. I asked the gentleman politely what his reason was for this offensive behaviour and he threatened to throw marmalade and butter at me as well. There was no provocation, sir. I stood where I stand now and have stood for the past twenty minutes, waiting for my bus to the south side."

"What you want me to do?" the flywheel of the law asks, lookin' first at the kid, then at me. He starts to withdraw his book an' a ballpoint pen from his pocket.

"Do? What can I do?" That little bastard was trowelin' it on now.

"Well, you can charge him with assault . . . He hit you with somethin' . . . That's what you said."

"Yes. With this loaf of bread. Do you wish to take it as evidence?"

"Naw . . . that won't be necessary. A description will suffice . . ." He was writin' now, slowly an' stiffly, the way a rookie writes when he can't spell too good. "One sixteen ounce loaf of McGavin's bread . . ."

"White bread," corrected the little bastard.

"White bread," he crosses out an' rewrites. "Now how were you hit with this . . . this projectile?"

"In the mouth!" I shouted down. The rookie points a law enforcement finger at me.

"You're not makin' the charge, so shut up!" he orders. Then he thinks of somethin' else.

"What's your name?"

"Joe King — son of MacKenzie King. He done it in the ladies' washroom at the Chateau Laurier after a Christmas party."

"Joe . . . King . . ." I'll be damned if he wasn't writin' it down. I started to laugh, loud, so the whole street could hear me. An' while they were conferrin' on the sidewalk under my window as to how to put me in the slammer, I filled a paper laundry bag at my sink with as much water as it would hold without tearin', then carefully I carried it over to the window. The rookie an' the university punk were now standin' close together, examinin' the way the cop had written out charges against me.

"Assault has two esses," the kid says. The cop spits an' starts erasin'.

"Did I leave one out? . . . Shit, I did . . . It's the pencil . . . sticks sometimes. You *think* you've written it right when it stuck an' you left somethin' important out!"

"Very good, sir. I thank you." The kid is grinnin' an' turns away from the cop. I lean over them with the bag an' let it drop.

"Timber!" I roar so loud the glass in my window rattles. Both of them look up half a second before the water bomb hits the rookie dead centre to the kisser. The bag bursts, an' both of them are soaked an' covered with pieces of wet paper.

"Goddamnit!" the cop swears. Just then, the bus the kid's been waitin' for arrives an' stops with a shoosh an' whistle of the brakes. The kid gets into the bus, an' it leaves. The cop brushes his tunic, picks up his hat an' plops it hard on his square block of a head. Then he pockets his book an' looks up at me, his face mad — red mad.

"Okay, you sonofabitch! I'm takin' you in!" An' he runs for the side door into the lobby.

Now I'm movin' fast too. Slammin' the window shut. Off with my shoes, socks, pants an' shirt. In my bedside table, top drawer, I keep a self-gummin' moustache matchin' the color of my hair. I slap it on sometimes after a wrestlin' match when I'm tired an' want to get away from all the middle-aged groupies crowdin' the ropes for a sniff of wrestle sweat. I whop this on my top lip an' dive for bed, pullin' the covers up to my chin.

One minute . . . two minutes pass. An' the expected knock comes at my door. Hard, hinge-breakin' — the knock of the law comin' with a big stick after a poor man who likes to have a laugh.

I wait a minute, throw myself from side to side in bed so's he can hear the bedsprings.

"Wha . . . eh? . . . Who is it?" I say in a hoarse, just-waking-up voice.

"It's the police! Open up, or I'll kick the goddamned door in!"

"Police? . . . What the hell!" I keep up the game, but now I put a bit of anger in my voice. "I'm in bed!"

"So's my grannie's poodle — open up!" He's wet, he's mad.

"Come in . . . door's unlocked!"

That always breaks a cop's pace — an unlocked door. Those bulls are used to everythin' being locked up like silverware belongin' to the Mafia. He opens the door slowly. then jumps in, his hand on his holster. I'm lyin' in bed, rubbin' my eyes. For a moment, he's not sure. You got to remember, this punk's only a rookie.

"Where's the other guy?" he asks.

"What other guy? I'm alone in here. What the hell is this — a faggot raid?" I'm soundin' pretty browned off by now. Throwin' my bare feet out of bed, I get up an' open the window, because the room's hot. "What time is it, amigo?"

It was a mistake gettin' out of bed. There's not many guys around built like me, an' seein' me upright, he begins to think somethin's not what it appears to be.

"You're him! You're the one!" He pulls out his charge book now an' flips through it, his hands shakin' with anger. The book's wet, an' the pages stick together. "Your name's Joe somethin' or other!"

"My name's Romco Kuchmir, you prick. What's all this about? What time is it?"

"Same time as yesterday at this time, only a day later." He's still goin' through his book.

Like I say, a cop's brain atrophies from the time he's twelve an' had his first wet dream. I could've got him goin' on a string of French-Canadian jokes if I phrased the next question right, but I didn't because I don't care for them jokes. There's lots of people here in the west who believe them. Put a ten-gallon hat on a Calgary businessman, set him up with some booze an' ten Newfie jokes an' you've got the next most deadly thing to an atom bomb goin' for you.

Oh, I know, I talk big an' bad sometimes. But if you ever tell my story, you tell it like I said it. Don't clean up anythin'. I am what I am because of the way I was born an' lived. I couldn't be different. I've done some good things because I'm human. The bad things, well, I'm comin' through the dark an' feelin' my way. If I make mistakes, I'm sure god will forgive me, even if some men can't. In heaven they will, because up there I'm gonna be a bartender!

So there's this rookie cop in my hotel room. He's beginnin' to see the light, but can't tell where it's comin' from.

"I'm arrestin' you for assault an' public mischief," he says to me.

"Hold it . . . now hold on!" I caution him, puttin' my hand on his shoulder, like a brother. "You come in here wakin' me up from a good sleep, lookin' for another guy. Now you're arrestin' me — why? Because you can't find the guy you're after. Is that the way a good city constable upholds the law?"

"Cut it out. I know it was *you*!" he says.

"Then would you shut your eyes an' describe whoever it was that was supposed to do whatever it was he did?" I spoke like a father to a son. He didn't know his limitations. I could see that from the way his eyes wandered around the room now.

"Okay. From an open window, a loaf of bread was thrown down to the street, strikin' an innocent bystander," he began.

"Hold it there!" I made out like I was excited by somethin' that just came to me. "My window was shut! You seen me open my window when you came in. What else?"

He was wilting.

"Here, have a chair." I moved him to where he could sit. "You walk through a fire hose or somethin'? You're wet. What did this . . . this bread thrower look like?"

"He looked like you."

"What kind of description is that — 'he looked like you'? Was he bare like me? Did he have a suit on? Glasses?"

"I . . . don't remember . . ."

"What color was his hair? Did he have a beard?"

"No, he didn't have a beard."

"Moustache then? What color?"

"He didn't have no moustache," the uniformed prick was startin' to quiver at the lip.

"He didn't have a moustache? You say he didn't have a moustache?" I raised my voice in fury an' he was movin' towards the door. "He didn't have a moustache, an' you come into my room like it was a public washroom, wake me, an' accuse me of assault. What in hell do you think this is growin' under my nose? An elevated cunt?"

"I . . . I'm sorry." He was puttin' his book away an' helplessly brushin' at his soppin' tunic. I stepped to the door an' threw it open.

"Never mind the sorry crap. You just get your ass out of here an' don't ever let me see you again or I'll have you up for harassin' an innocent man!"

He could see by my face the last word had been spoken. Quickly, he left my room an' marched down the hallway, his pointed head bobbin', his shoulders hunched.

"Hey!" I called after him. "Watch out so a sack of water don't fall on you again! It might sprain your neck next time!"

He stops in his tracks an' spins around. But I was starin' at him like I was just offerin' some good advice which had come to me. He wasn't sure if I was shaftin' him or not, an' being only a rookie, he wasn't chancin' false arrest. I shut the door, an' this time I locked it.

Yeh, I like razzin' cops. Started in my boyhood. There was a cafe around the corner from my old man's poolhall. Cops used to go there for coffee. In the winter they drank a helluva lot of coffee just to stay out of the cold. A bunch of us punks would be out lookin' for trouble, especially after it got dark outside. We'd carry two blocks of twelve by twelve, cut from ends of timbers.

I was built like a brick shithouse from the time I was fourteen. I'd grab the cops' car by the back bumper, liftin' it while two other guys slipped the blocks under the wheel housings. Then we'd heave a handful of gravel against the cafe window, right beside where the cops sat. Bingo! They're on their feet an' runnin for the door. We're off like shots down the street. They're out of the restaurant an' into their car. We're behind some trees that aren't lit, an' we're watchin' as they rev the engine, throw the car in gear an' let the clutch in, twistin' the steerin' wheel at the same time. But they're not goin' anywhere . . . the suspended wheels howl as they pick up pebbles an' fire them like bullets across the parkin' lot, across the street.

Sometimes they'd catch a kid an' rough him up for it, but it was never a kid who did it.

Why did I do it? Because the guys who became cops were refugees from the same street corners an' dried out barley fields as I was. Those on top always use the poor to hit the poor. Givin' them a uniform kept them from bustin' windows an' tellin' the world they was alive, strong, horny an' needin' things. These cops were told they now served the queen. Not the banks, or railroads, or even people, but a queen who wouldn't know if Wetaskiwin, Alberta was in the Sudan or in the Northwest Territories! Those punks wouldn't know a queen if they caught her liftin' panty-hose at Woolworth's.

"I am her majesty, your queen!"

"Throw her in the slammer! Some kooky broad. Imagine

. . . Wearin' a trike wheel rim on her head in July! Some damned middle-aged hippie, that's all she is — throw her in the slammer!''

The more ridiculous the symbol, the easier to believe in it. Always been that way. Thousands . . . tens of thousands of young punks long ago died in Palestine. Walked all across Europe in their iron overcoats to get there, crossin' mountains, sinkin' in rivers, clawin' through mud an' over rockpiles — for what? To find an' bring home a fuckin' cup for their king! Not only that, but they killed off more Turks than are alive today because someone said the Turks had this cup an' were keepin' it for themselves!

Knowin' that, an knowin' cops don't bake bread or grease up electric generators, I look at a cop an' laugh.

I don't do much that's useful either. But I've learned to live with that, findin' pieces of myself wherever they've been left. That's a pretty fulltime job in itself, my friend.

Don't you agree?

seven

Yeah, I've managed women wrestlers. They're just ordinary kids tryin' to make some bread. But they get pushed around a lot. They draw big in isolated minin' towns an' oil rig camps, where there's few broads comin' through. So that's where I take them. But I also take along a three-foot long lead pipe when I go.

Holdin' this lead pipe in my hand, I announce some ground rules before my wrestlers come on.

"This here pipe's full of lead. Any guy reachin' through the ropes when the ladies are rasslin' gets it across the knuckles. An' at the hotel tonight, they're sleepin' in back of my room. If you want to take your chances gettin' past me, it's your funeral they'll be holdin' on Wednesday, not mine."

To give my words a little more carryin' power, I suddenly lift the pipe an' swing it against the iron ring post, puttin' a buckle in it where none had been before. That's enough to make even the toughest cat-skinner quiet an' respectful when I bring the women out. An' only twice, if I'm careful to assert who's boss, have I had to throw punks down the staircase of a hotel.

Still, broads who wrestle get pushed around when there's nobody to help them. There's a type of guy who really gets his jollies from watchin' broads throw each other around. He's usually a small guy who sits in corners listenin' to what drinkin' men say to each other. But he drinks by himself, one glass of brandy for the whole night. He usually dresses well an' don't mix much. All I know about what goes on in his head is what I've had one of them tell me. He could've lied for all I know.

He worked in the post office an' grew begonias in his kitchen. After one match I promoted for the women, he comes up to me, offerin' three hundred bucks if I would fix him up with Lindy-Lou, one of the tougher gals I had workin' for me that time.

"What do you take me for — a pimp?" I says to him.

"No sir, I'm not suggesting that, heaven forbid. I want ... an introduction an' a chance to be alone with her for two hours. I've got money. I can pay whatever it'll cost."

I bored hard into him with my eye, but he didn't budge. He just looked back at me, his pale blue eyes innocent an' pleadin'.

"What's with you? What is it you're lookin' for?"

He shrugged an' bit his lips, but said nothing.

"Look, I've been around. I've known guys who'd steal a broad's shoe or a piece of clothin' an' sleep with it like a kid with a toy bear. Guys like that have pimples, or wide noses. You're not like that. You're not after an ordinary date like a gentleman, or you'd ask her yourself. How do you see her? What in hell is it that turns you on enough to come to me with a request to hustle for you?"

He cleared his throat an' nodded for me to follow him. We began walkin' nowhere in particular. The smell of sweat in the arena hung like smoke in the air.

"I don't know ... there's something about her ... somethin' free an' strong out of another world I can only think about. I don't want to jump into bed with her ... it's not like that at all," he says.

"No, I didn't think you would."

"There's a strength an' roughness about her that I can't escape ... I've tried, but I can't escape. I imagine she goes to her room at night, an' goes to bed with ... black undies an' jackboots. That she phones down for a man like she'd ordered a cheese sandwich. I'd pay anythin' ... just to see ... bring something for her ... say hello ..."

"You don't want to touch her?"

"No . . . I just want to see her, that's all!" There was somethin' whinin' an' desperate in his voice now. I stopped walkin' an' turned him roughly by the shoulder to face me.

"You came here tonight to see her fight. Why?" I shouted an' shook him.

"Because I believe in her! She's got the sort of strength for which I'd do anything she asked!"

"Even kill?"

"Yes." The word came out of him in a whimper.

"Like for the queen of a country . . . or for a goddess?"

"Yes!"

I pushed him away. Not roughly, just enough to let him know there was nothin' more to be said. I told Lindy-Lou about his proposition when we got back to the hotel. The part about him worshipping her bothered me, an' I told her all about it. That tough little broad takes out a pair of scissors an' starts clippin' her toenails while I'm talkin'.

"I've never known a man who'd say that," I'm tellin' her. "Wonder how it happened? Maybe somethin' got turned around when he was a boy."

"Fuckin' creep," she says like we were discussin' a fly fallin' in her soup. She keeps on cuttin' her toenails, her leg muscles showin' up like rope pulled tight under the skin. I look at her a long while, my eyes half-shut so I'm not seein' her, just feelin' for the atmosphere around her. She's a strong broad, not easy to sit with in a room.

"Creeps like that should be put away an' the keys thrown out the window." She's still cuttin' her toenails.

"I feel kind of sorry for him. That's not much to live for," I says. I can feel her lookin' at me now.

"Not me. Any guy who looks at me that way gets his face pushed in!"

An' damned if I didn't get a glimmer of what it was that had trapped my friend from the post office, who grew begonias in his kitchen. But I'm put together different than him, an' that sort of thing don't excite me. In fact, I had to leave her room halfway through my beer, because I knew what I came to find out, an' her toeclippin' was startin' to make me mad.

Broads who wrestle for a livin' got my respect. They're serious an' work very hard at it. The crackerjacks in the racket are the midgets!

You book two midgets on a card an' you've got nothin' but trouble from the moment they arrive in town until they leave. They're built the same way you an' I are built . . . normal size heads an' dinks — the two things that matter. The rest of them's a bit haywire, but that's alright. I've never known a midget on welfare, have you?

There's one of these pint-sized boomers who calls himself the Nevada Strangler. Little bastard comes from High Prairie an' his name's Swinbourne. But that's alright with me. A name like Nevada Strangler gets you more bookings than High Prairie Choker. He's spunky as hell, an' I'm bookin' him for next November if we don't have a depression first. He's spunky. I seen him tryin' to take on Gorgeous George on the sidewalk just outside that door. George says to him that a midget's got a lopsided view of broads. The height he stands at, all he can see is the woman's crotch. When he speaks to a broad, that's what he says "Good mornin'" to! An' "Good night," an' "How're you doin', kid? How's tricks?" . . .

George says to him that with this altered perspective, the questions take on another meanin', that it's bound to warp the minds of little men. That there's more to broads if only the Strangler would stand up on a stool sometimes an' take a look at other parts than those at the height of his nose.

This little boomer's been drinkin' a bit, an' all of a sudden he takes objection to the big wrestler.

"You insulted me! You apologize to me right now!" He's red faced an' yellin'. An old Indian carryin' a cardboard suitcase is passin' by at that moment. He stops to pat the Strangler on the head.

"Kinda late to be on the street, li'l boy," he says in a father-Indian kind of way. "You better get on home before your mommy gets sore . . . or worried."

"Fuck you in the earhole, daddy!" says the "li'l boy" to the old Indian, who looks down at him with the sad old face of a grocer who'd just found mice in his flour shed.

"You white kids gone all to hell," he says an' walks away. Gorgeous George is laughin', an' the Strangler is still lookin' for satisfaction.

"You apologize like I asked!" He's bleatin' like a billy-goat.

"Apologize? What the hell for? When you're mad like that, you look like a bantam rooster, you know that?"

The midget starts rollin' up the sleeves of his little boy shirt. His eyes have gone kind of hard an' small now.

"I'm gonna kick the hell out of you if you don't tell me you're sorry!"

The big wrestler's sittin' on the edge of the sidewalk, his legs way out into the street. Even so, the Strangler only came up to his shoulders. But damn if he doesn't take a run at Gorgeous George, his fists goin' like a mill, feet kickin' into the ribs of the blonde giant. George puts up his hand an' shoves the midget away. But he's back, chargin' again an' again, like a bull against a haystack.

George gets to his feet, an' reachin' out, grabs the Strangler by the back of the shirt. He puts him under his arm, like a duffle bag.

"Hell, Swinbourne, I came out for some fresh air. What you got against the big people, anyway? What's got into you?" he says, as he walks into the hotel.

"You'll burn for this! You'll hear from my lawyer! Don't think you've heard the last of this one! You'll know who you've tangled with before I'm finished with you . . ." He's fightin' all the way as the big wrestler carries him upstairs an' to his room.

An hour later, he's in fresh trouble with a broad who's

called down to the desk to complain about him. The call's transferred to my room, as I'm responsible for the little bugger so long's he's in the vicinity of greater Edmonton. I promised the cops that.

"Yeh . . . what's up?" I ask.

"I'm charging him with indecent exposure!" The broad on the other end of the line is sore.

"Don't do nothin', I'm on the way. Which room you in?"

"Three-nineteen," she says an' hangs up.

I go up to the third floor, an' there's the Strangler runnin' up an' down the hallway, naked except for a small towel he's wrapped around his bottom like a diaper. He's had a shower, his hair is still wet.

"What are you up to? You want to get us all in the slammer? Or thrown out on the street? Jesus, you're like a stuck jack-hammer! Get your clothes on. What room you in?" I was mad at him for makin' trouble.

"I don't remember . . . I want my mudder!"

An' he's off down the hallway at a run. I come after him, but damned if I could catch him. Them stubby little legs of his were like two little bangers, goin' to beat hell. At the end of the hallway, he's through the fire door an' goin' down the stairs to the second floor. I've got difficulty runnin' down stairs — right leg sometimes buckles under me, so I was delayed gettin' to the landing. When I pushed the hallway door open, I was worked up enough to nail him against the ceiling once I'd caught him.

But now he'd found himself a friend — a woman about fifty with a bust this big! The kind whose name an' picture appears in newspapers as co-ordinator of fund drives for the benefit of things that are sick, lame or poor. She's holdin' him around the neck, an' bugger him if he isn't snugged up against her, his nose in her crotch.

"I want my mudder!" he's wailin' an' snortin' through his nose. Without lookin', he's pointin' at me. "That's a bad man that one, missus. Gave me two candies, an' said there was more in his room. Took my clothes off an' took me to the shower with him. I want my mudder!"

"Swinbourne!" I roars at him. "I've left a bond with the cops to get you in. If I lose that money, I'm gonna kill you!"

The woman gives me a stare that would frost the tit on a saint.

"You degenerate old animal! Shame on you!" she snaps at me.

"I want my mudder. I gotta wee-wee!" He's at it again, jumpin' up an' down now an' crossin' his legs over one another.

"Swinbourne! . . ."

"Go away! Men like you belong in cages!" She's a defender of little boys now, all the furies of hell together with a strong dose of presbyterian righteousness burning in her eyes.

"Myehh!" says the little bastard, using every advantage he's got. She's all mother all of a sudden as she pets the monster on the head.

"You poor child, come with me. I'll help you . . . There now . . . There's a place to wee-wee in my room! Come along."

She opens her door an' leads the way in, the Strangler hangin' on to her skirt. The door shuts. I take a few paces so I'm opposite the door. Then facing it, I lean against the wall, my hands in my pockets. All I have to do now is wait . . .

I don't have to wait long. Ten seconds maybe. There's one helluva commotion in the room. A door bangs open an' shuts. She's yellin' something, then I hear her clear sayin', "No, you stop that! Please — I'm not kiddin'. You do that again an' I'm gonna scream! Get out . . . You bastard!"

I heard the midget laughin', then I hear a lamp fall an' break. He lets out a "yippee!" an she screams.

"You ever seen one like that before, eh? It's a prize,

ain't it?" he says, an' laughs again.

I don't hear anymore after that, because now the door's thrown open, an' out comes the Strangler, naked an' stumblin' to regain his balance. The woman's right behind him, her skirt twisted, hair mussed up. She throws the towel after him. Her face is red an' she's breathin' hard. Then she sees me.

"You!" she hollers as she points a finger at me. The finger has two rings, an' the nail is painted the same red color you see on new barn shingles. "You . . . set him up to this! Admit it!"

"Lady," I says, "when I first seen you, I was tryin' to apprehend this monster from doin' what he did. It was you who stopped me takin' him."

"I want my mudder!" The Strangler's at it again, stampin' his foot an' chewin' on his towel.

"Swinbourne," I says to him in as casual a voice as I could muster. "You stop that right now or I'm gonna kick your butt right out the top of your head!"

"No, you won't! *I* will!" says the dowager queen from the fund raisin' committees. I agreed, an' we parted on that, me bowin' to her from the hip like a perfect gentleman, an' she slammin' the door in my face while I'm doin' my bit for peace an' understandin'.

"Hey, that was a pretty good bit of fun. Let's go do it some more . . ."

I didn't let him finish what he was sayin'. Because the moment that door shut, I had that little bastard by the hair an' my other fist up against his nose.

"One more word, Swinbourne, an' you're gettin' this! Then I'm takin' you to your room an' puttin' you inside, where you'll stay until your bus leaves town!"

"I've locked myself out," he says.

"Don't worry. We'll break the door open . . . with your head!"

As it turned out, the midget never locked any door

through which he came or went. What could he lose? What sort of person would enter a room an' remove a little boy suit? Or a pair of little boy shoes?

I've known them all in the wrestling game. Pete the Swede, the broken-nosed, flop-eared, pot-bellied old prize fighter who turned to wrestlin' for retirement money. The day I met Pete was the day I decided to promote rather than fight. You keep fightin' an' eventually you get to look a bit like him. Then where in hell are you?

No broad wants to go to bed with a face like that, even if she's paid to do it. An' the day I pay for tail is the day I want you to put a rope aroun' my neck an' take me to some little meadow where there's crows cawin' an' nobody to see. I'll dig my own grave. An' when I'm done, I want you to shoot me, push me down the hole an' cover me. In a meadow where there's only crows an' magpies. It's worse than havin' a disease for which there's no cure, livin' like that.

Hey! What is worse — havin' a chronic bladder infection, or carryin' a criminal record? You don't know? Well, I'll tell you if you don't know. You can't leave the country or work for the post office with a record. You can't even work as a dog catcher, because that's government work. A leaky bladder is your own personal problem, but time in the slammer is everybody's business.

I learned all that from Klondike Karl, who had that kind of infection. He told me he got it in the war, but I never asked how. You never asked that bushman anythin' that couldn't be answered with a grunt.

It'd be forty below outside an' you know what he'd do to attract attention? He'd go out with no jacket, his shirt sleeves rolled up, barefoot an' lickin' an ice-cream cone! Whenever I booked him for a fight, I didn't need posters or TV publicity. All I had to do was bring him in three days before a fight durin' the coldest part of winter, park him in front of the hotel for an hour each evening, an' he'd fill the house night of the match!

But I did that only when I was flat. If I had the loot, I kept him out of town because when he was here, he insisted on stayin' with me in my room. He wasn't the best kind of dinner companion, I'll tell you. When I'd take him out for a steak, he insisted they only warm it up in the pan. He'd take this slab of raw meat in his hands an' eat it like he was a fuckin' coyote!

"Why don't you order a moose lung next time?" I says to him one evening when he'd put me off any eating. "It's slippery an' goes down without chewin'."

"Yah. But it gives you gas!"

In my room he'd jump for the phone any time it rang, an' answer all my calls, his ugly mug all happy, because nobody ever phoned *him*.

"Hullo! . . . Speak up you sonofabitch — I can't hear you! Yah, sure . . . he's here. What for you want to talk to him? Listen . . . anythin' you got to say to my boss you can say to me — we're just like that, him an' me!" . . .

By the time I tore the phone out of his mitt, I stood a fifty-fifty chance of losin' a backer. A social caller had usually hung up by then.

He couldn't read time, an' one night when I'd parked him in front of the hotel barefoot in the snow, I went in an placed a long distance call to a bim in Florida, forgettin' all about him. It was an hour an' forty-five minutes later that I remembered he was still there. When I went out to call him in, his feet had froze to the pavement. The last guy who worked on your job an' I worked for ten minutes pourin' warm water over his feet, before we thawed him loose. After that, he wore these Jesus-big padded caribou moccasins when he went out.

"Sometimes you're no good, Romeo," he says to me. "You get too busy an' forget about friends you got workin' for you. In the Klondike, you don't telephone another friend when you've got one already!''

An' you know, to this day I'm not sure if he was the best actor I met or whether he looked that hurt for real as he stared at me with them yellow timberwolf eyes of his. It got to me, right in the heart. An' after that I never treated Klondike Karl the same way I treat other wrestlers.

Mind you, I didn't book him too much either. He was hard to take more than one time a year.

eight

I would like to be a good man. A man people love an' look up to. But I was born an' raised in the shadow of a poolhall. Even though I loved my mother — an' I loved her in ways I can't explain, where I grew up, a woman was a broad. A noisy man was the leader of a gang. So I talk an' think like I was trained to do.

I've loved as many women as there's stars in the sky. An army of women, enough to settle a small city. Fat women, thin ones, old, young, white, black an' yellow. No remorse. Only hope that life gives me more of the same. The root of a man is democratic as hell . . . Class an' color mean nothin'. Reason is the enemy. Wake up in the mornin', an' she's puttin' on a face for other people, mostly men.

"Hey, let's stay here a week! I hear birds in the trees. Everything's laughin'!"

"Yes, Romeo, it was beautiful. But we must be reasonable. If my family or friends knew of this, my job is finished and so is my integrity."

I laughed. But she dressed her body like it was made of ice, an' pretty soon, I wasn't laughin' anymore.

I once knew a broad who was as moral as Saint Peter's gatekeeper. She once says to me that Bertrand Russell was a "marvellous man", except that he slept with many women. Which wasn't moral in her eyes. One curiosity cancels out another, an' that's that. I went to the library an' got a book by Bertrand Russell. I read it slow, tastin' every word. Right from the first page I understood — an' she didn't — that the old man's brain an' cock were part of the same body. The brilliant man an' the lover were the same person. That neither god nor the devil had any special privileges once the old man's motors were started up an' goin'.

This same moral broad was a swimmer. A good swimmer — Olympic calibre stuff. She'd invite city workin' girls to the pool to give them instructions on how to dive an' swim — but only once. The next time they wanted to come, they'd have to pay money to join a club she owned.

"That's immoral!" I shout at her when she tells me. "A talent like you got is a gift from god himself! Share it with the poor. It's no fault of hers that some broad was born more stupid than you, goddamn you!"

An' you know what she says to me?

"I wish you wouldn't swear," she says. "I'm not arguin' with you. It's undignified to argue with someone who swears an' shouts like an animal."

She turns on her heel an' walks away from me. She's a rich little broad today, owns two health spas an' goes on African safaris in September with punks in the jet set. I never went to bed with her . . . I couldn't. I can screw a whore an' laugh with joy. But I can't screw an immoral woman.

I couldn't hold a marriage together, kid. Even though I could help any friend I had with his or her marriage. But not for myself, not for me. Because the woman I married also grew up in the shadow of a poolhall. We inherited each other, like a family, or an old book full of faded pictures. There were no surprises. Only the same memories. I didn't want them memories comin' at me like a winter frost, an' me standin' around in a summer jacket.

"You've spent more on telephone calls than I've spent on rent an' groceries, Romeo," she says. "And your clothes . . . I seen a suit on sale for forty dollars that I could've taken in to fit you."

A good woman, but with a touch of death in the way she spoke an' moved. *My* death. Then the kid was born, but even that was a piss-off. Lots of talcum powder an' oil, an' the juices of life dryin'; her rubbin' her left eye more an' more until I'd have to leave the house an' go somewhere quiet to cry.

An' you know somethin' else, kid? There's no end to it. When I get old an' fitted with porcelain teeth an' a walkin' stick, I'll go back to her. I'll have to go home to die with her. She knows that, an' she's waitin'. Like a hungry crow on a barbwire fence, she's waitin'.

Why do I depress you an' myself with such thoughts? There's an hour of the night, maybe the hour of night we'll die, when we start thinkin' about how we become less than we might've been.

Take me — a man. A lot of time was spent — a million years an' a lot of reckonin' by the master Manmaker how to put me together. Good eyes an' ears, this bone attached to that one. The heart an' lungs just so . . . Feet that run, an' an elbow that's the right height for leanin' on a bar! Eh? Then after so many years, most of them spent learnin' how to speak an' walk without fallin', I die. An' I'm put in the ground, like a sack of carrots. An' from the ground I push up grass which some prick with a lawnmower cuts an' rakes away as so much rubbish. That's my blood an' bones an' brains he's rakin' away — but does he care?

Or worse still, a dumb Holstein cow comes over me an' eats me up. An' everything I was is reduced to one lump of cowshit an' a pint of milk, which can be worked down by some dairy genius into half an ounce of sour cheese!

So . . . after all them millions of years, I become a bit of cheese which someone eats in one swallow while he's worryin' if his car will start!

Yet . . . I'm optimistic. Yesterday, I seen a young broad with a baby come into the hotel. While I'm standin' around, she registers for a room. Then she goes into the restaurant. I follow her, an' sit at the table beside her. She doesn't know I'm there. She opens her blouse an' gives her baby a tit to suck. There's the kid, drinkin' her life an' strength, it's little arms goin' this way an' that, while she's rockin' in her chair and softly singin'. An' I think to myself — it's a goddamn miracle, that's what it is — all this givin' an' takin'.

I know who I love. An' I know who I'll marry . . .

It will take another seven or eight months for that little bugger to get up on its feet an' stand without fallin' . . . a trick the calf or colt learns in the first day of life.

But fifteen years from now, that kid will forget the difficulty of standin' up. It will be sittin' in school doin' physics. While the goddamn horse will still only have learned how to use its feet. That's a miracle, an' it's happening millions of times every day all over the world! What's wrong with us that we can't be grateful for this miracle we call life? That we can still take food away from starvin' children? An' kill other lives like our own for a piece of extra soil, or a political difference of opinion that is of no help at all growing a crop of potatoes or an apple tree!

I had a friend who was a killer. His name was Blackball Stinsman. He prospected an' he trapped — the only occupations left which had no respect for property boundaries or the right to life of other species. Blackball would go through your house lawn if he thought he'd find gold there. An' in the bush, anythin' that moved got shot.

It got shot because it had fur he could skin an' sell for money. What was left, he an' his dog, Hurricane, ate. Stinsman stood a good six inches taller than me. An' the dog, who was part wolf, came up to my belt buckle. So between the two of them they could put away a lot of porcupines, squirrels, deer shanks an' muskrats in a winter. When he came into town from his hunt an' prospect, the dog an' Blackball took a room together. Then they'd throw the hotel window open an' roar. Blackball roared because he'd generally had a bottle of rye whiskey an' had started on a second an' was feelin' pretty good. The dog roared for the hell of it.

"When I go through the bush I kick the trees until they shake so they fuckin' well know that I'm alive an' comin' through!" he says, spittle flyin' out of his bearded big mouth, his eyes blinkin' hard with every word, which was spoken at full voice.

"I heard you, I heard you! Goddamn, but a man has to have an umbrella talkin' to you!"

"What's wrong with my talkin'?" he hollers at me.

"Your teeth are goin'," I says to him. "An' becuase you never learned to speak normal, you're drivin' a shower of spit when you make a speech. Why don't you see a dentist?"

"What the hell for?"

"You'll never be a good-lookin' man, but you can cut back a bit on the ugly," I says. "An' have a bath some-time. You an' your damned dog smell the same!"

He started laughin' then — a wild man's laugh rattlin' the windows an' goin' right through the hotel like a loose water pipe.

"I lift my arms an' everybody in the house is runnin' for cover, eh? Not like you, Kuchmir, with the sweet whore perfume, not like you! But who's got more money, you or me? Come on, guess!"

He puts down the whiskey bottle an' digs into his pockets with both hands, pullin' out two huge wads tied with twine. He drops the money on the bed.

"There it is — twenty grand, my son! I can buy anythin' with twenty grand — whiskey, a rifle, hotel rooms, nooky. Even if I never have a bath. I just drop the cash on the table an' holler. 'Gimme!'" If it don't come to me like that, I take the money back. If you've got more money than me — show me!"

"Naw. You win. I'm busted. Maybe you can make me a loan. You don't need money doin' what you're doin'. So give it to me an' I'll spend it in a civilized way."

Again, he laughs. The dog bares his teeth, hops on the

window ledge with his front paws scrapin' the glass an' lets out an excited howl towards the street.

"Take it from me!" Blackball shouts. "There it is on the bed — wrestle me for it! Kill me for it. Kill my dog too. *I'd* kill for twenty grand! I'd kill a man, his wife an' his kids for it, then burn his house down with everybody in it! But I'm leavin' with the stuff that buys everythin'!"

"Get yourself a woman for the night. You're bushed," I says to him.

He got sort of thoughtful then.

"Naw. I can't do it, son."

"Why not? You been through a bad frost with your pants down?"

"Well, if someone was to fix me up, he'd have to fix up Hurricane here as well. We been together a long time. Wouldn't be fair me funnin' an' him sittin' outside the door, listenin'."

"It was a friendly suggestion, that's all. But the deal's off." I says. "I'm not pimpin' for your goddamn dog, that's for sure."

"Don't say that. It puts him off. He's sensitive, you know. If I moved a finger now, he'd take your arm off for sayin' that. He's like people, Romeo. He laughs sometimes, you know."

"Laughs?"

"Yeh, he likes fun. Same's me! One evening, we're out in the bush. I've been trackin' this bull moose, whose ass I've shot off but can't bring him down. Hurricane wants to take him, but I hold him back. No, this one's mine. The moose is mad with pain. They've got very small brains, the moose. But when one has a grudge, he'll get you. This one I'm shootin' has a grudge the size of a warehouse."

"I get him out into a clearin'. His back end is all bloodied. He's makin' angry sounds an' tossin' his head from side to side as he turns to me. I put my rifle down beside a tree an' rip off a sheet of birch bark. Then I take my lighter out, an' sheet of birch back in one hand an' Ronson lighter in the other, I step out into the clearin' . . .''

"Come on, you sonofabitch! . . . You can get me if luck's on your side . . . Come on!' I'm shoutin'. He tosses his horns again, lowers his head an' starts to paw up ground. Hurricane yelps, an' I turn to look at him. The dog's grinnin'. He knows the odds an' he's enjoyin it, same's me!''

"Then suddenly, the goddamn moose charges. He's comin' straight for me, enough weight there to pulverize a C.P.R. station! I stand where I am, legs wide apart, hootin'. "Come on, you sonofabitch! It's you an' me now! No guns, just you against me!''

"When he's only yards away, hot an' troubled so I can smell his need to kill, I flick the lighter an' bring it over to the birch bark I'm holdin' in the other hand. I hold my breath as it sputters, then catches fire, fast.''

"'Ha!' I holler at the top of my voice an' run towards the moose with the birch bark torch held in front of me. There's a look in his eyes as he comes to a quick stop — panic, pain . . . death. Just that glimmer of intelligence before the end that tells him he's lost, that I'll kill him now on my own terms, in my own way. He lets out this terrible cry an' turns. But he's not runnin', not doin' anything except breathin' heavy. I back away an' pick up my rifle.''

"The look on my dog's face is the happiest thing I ever seen. I lift up the rifle an' blow out the heart an' lungs of that moose at point-blank range. Hurricane lets out a yclp an' he's grinnin' from ear to ear. Because he knows he's on the winnin' side again.''

"What if . . . the lighter . . . hadn't lit?'' I asked.

Blackball stared at me as if I was speakin' some language he didn't understand. Hurricane was also starin' at me, with the same expression. Then the dog barked at me, an' Blackball threw his head back an' laughed.

"What if the lighter hadn't lit? . . . Eh, Hurricane? Did you hear that? . . . What would've happened if the lighter hadn't lit?" He laughed some more, then, suckin' in the contents of his nose with a burbling noise, he rises to his feet, goes to open the window, an' spits out what he's sucked down.

"I'd of been killed dead if that lighter hadn't lit, that's what would've happened!"

"Pick up your money an' put it away," I says to him.

"Why?"

"Somethin' about you an' money makes me nervous. Like life an' death rentin' a hotel room together."

"You think I'm crazy, don't you, Kuchmir?" he asks me quietly, very seriously.

"You've no respect for life. You're like that dog of yours — kill anythin' to survive."

"Nope. He's grinnin' when I'm takin' chances. If that moose had rammed me to kingdom come, you know what Hurricane would've done?"

"No."

"Eaten me up. Just like he ate what I left of that moose. I'm different than Hurricane. I kill. He stands around, his tongue hangin' out, waitin' for someone else to kill for him. He's more like you than me, Kuchmir! He grins because he's probably heard of Jesus Christ an' the ten commandments. Someone might've read a book to him once on how to set things up so they work for you, even when you're sleepin'!"

There was a strange look comin' over Blackball's face which I didn't like.

"Leave the dog here an' come with me, Stinsman. I'm buyin' you a drink, an' then I'll fix you up with a degenerate sailor who'll suck your eyeballs dry!" I tried to cheer him up like that. But he wasn't listening. He scooped up his money an' shoves it into his jacket pocket. Then he goes to the door an' looks both ways along the hallway.

"Yeh, that's what it's all about," he says, an' closes the door. Hurricane is nervous now, movin' towards the window. But Blackball is there ahead of him, an' slammin' the window down hard. Hurricane is whinin' an' lickin' his lips with fear.

"Come on, Blackball — let's go!" I says to him.

"Yeh — now I understand!" He pushes me aside an', hunching over, follows the dog. "I step out into the world in hobnailed boots. I shoot anythin' that's movin', kick in doors of trappers' cabins, rip the guts out of mountain creeks, lookin' for gold. Another man like me comes too near an' I shoot his drinkin' cup out of his hand. Nobody takes Blackball Stinsman — I holler every mornin'! Nobody gets a free fuck on me! I don't ask for a fixed address or a pension plan. When I get sick, I either get better by myself or die. An' if I get too old to take care of myself, I'll always keep a spare shell in my rifle to choose the day an' the place I put a stop to gettin' older!"

"Cut it out, for Christ's sake! You're sprayin' spit like a rain machine. The dog's scared of you. You're gonna wake up the whole hotel. This isn't the bush, Blackball. It's night time in the city, man!" I try arguin' with him, because he's goin' queer on me.

"Yeah . . . Now I understand everything there's to know . . ."

He's crossin' the room this way an' that. An' the dog is dodging, his tail between his long wolf legs, teeth bared in panic, eyes never off the face of his owner.

"Never ask, or you got to give! For twenty years I've been an outlaw, killin' enough game to start a packin' plant of me own. I also killed three men who got in my way. They was victims an' evidence. I burned two of them to ashes in fires I cut poplars down to make, the third one went down the river with the spring runoff. If you've got a job to do, do it right by doin' it yourself, I always say! I never voted, never dressed up to go to a party. The first an' the last free man on earth. Twenty years of this, an' half an hour with a wrestler who's become a bum turns the world I know to shit!"

The old bastard is ragin' now, froth bubblin' on his lips. I'm gettin' worried, because there's a smell in the room I don't know — like somethin' you taste when you've been hit hard in the mouth.

"What the hell's wrong with you? You're gonna give yourself a heart attack. Let's get out of here!" I reached for his arm, but he whacked me across the wrist with his other hand, an' I was surprised at how strong he was. It hurt, but I wasn't goin' to show pain.

"You start gettin' rough with me, Stinsman, an' I'll put you in the hospital." It was a bluff, you know. I couldn't put him anywhere if he'd taken me on. But he wasn't listenin' . . .

"A dog . . . A goddamned, louse-infested, stinkin', piss-legged dog is usin' me! What the mounties couldn't find, what yankee minin' companies couldn't touch, my *soul*, this thing has eaten an' turned to wolf fart when I wasn't lookin'! I'm killin' him, Kuchmir!"

I sat down in a chair an' lit a cigarette. There's things a civilized man who goes to see opera an' ballet doesn't meddle in. I sat in a chair an' watched Blackball Stinsman an' the dog circle each other, both of them growlin'. The dog was the first to snap. He comes at Blackball fast an' hard, his claws rippin' through the front of the prospector's jacket an' shirt like it was paper, opening long cuts on his chest. At the same time, his jaws snapped at the man's head. Blackball ducked, but I saw that Hurricane had taken off half of his left ear, which he chewed once or twice an' dropped on the carpet. Just as quick as he'd attacked, the dog jumped back.

Blackball was movin' more quickly now, his nose drippin' with pain. His eyes were no longer those of a man. He was a wild animal, bent over, his hands curved like claws which cut through the air, openin' an' shutting as he moved closer an' closer to the dog, who slung away behind a sofa. It was like a dance — Blackball liftin' one end of the sofa an' throwin' it aside. The dog cornered, his teeth bared from nostrils to bottom gums.

Blackball let out a cry, more like a howl, and was on him. Bits of fur an' animal spittle flew across the lampshade as the dog threw his head from side to side, his legs rippin' at Blackball's body, then at air. For the prospector now had him around the throat an' was shakin' him like a piece of cloth.

"Lucifer or Jesus Christ . . . whichever! . . . You're dead now!" he says in a thick voice.

In a moment it was over. The hot smell of killer animals was nauseating an' everywhere in the room. Blackball pulled the dead body of Hurricane to the window. He opened the window, then reconsidered an' let the dog drop to the floor. Cool air blew into the room, cool an' sweet like the breath of a livin' garden. Blackball rested at the open window for a long while, breathin' hard an' noisy.

"Wash up an' I'll bring you some clothes," I says to him. "Then we'll go out an' have that drink."

"No."

"If anybody sees you like this, they'll take you away to the cuckoo farm, you crazy bastard. Once you're in there, you'll never get out. You're out of your head, you know that."

"Sure, I know," he agrees with me but doesn't move away from that window. I try to cheer him up a little.

"I once knew a guy who had a third cousin who got himself caught screwin' a Jersey cow. He got put away, Blackball. Nobody could get him out again. We even arranged for a letter from the cow, sayin' she didn't mind, that she kind of liked it the times he used a solid step-ladder. It was the other times when he used an upsidedown milk bucket that made her nervous . . ."

But Blackball was reachin' for his cap an' pushin' past me for the door.

"Cut out the shit, Kuchie. Get me a cab for the airport. I'm leavin' this town," he says. An' that was the last time I seen him.

He stays in my head, kid. The older I get, the more I find him inside my memories, especially when I read the newspapers. When I read about all them politicians who steal, or lawyers who lie defendin' men who kill thousands of people slowly, with poisoned food an' untested drugs, cars which fall apart, an' television sets that castrate you an' then burn your house down . . .

The worst time is when I see a baby suckin' its mother an' somethin' about that makes me think of Blackball Stinsman. That's scary. Because when that happens, I don't know what's brought it on or what it means. I'm a simple man. If I met Freud, I'd throw him in the crapper because if a man can't express himself simply so the whole world understands, then he's got nothin' worth listenin' to.

nine

Me father was hung for sheep stealin'
Me mother is grey-haired an' poor
Me brother is set up in business
Procurin' for bikers next door . . .

You should learn to sing songs like that at five in the mornin'. It beats stumblin' around in the dark lookin' for a sink to spit the taste of sleep into.

In the mornings, my uncle Vladimir used to open his eyes an' say, "Another day, another dollar!"

Which woke my aunt Sophie beside him. She opened her eyes, looked at him an' said, "Thank God, another day closer to death."

On the outskirts of my town, there was a coalshed when I was a kid. One winter, my old man's poolhall wasn't payin' for what we ate. So the old man built me a sled. It was built of pine with a plank deck on top. He attached a long rope to the runners.

"Go steal some coal, like a good boy," he says to me. "If the police catch you, say it was a joke. No, better still, say it's for the widow Hughes down the street. It makes you a thief. It also makes you a good boy."

So I haul this sleigh out when it's dark, six empty burlap sacks, the sled an' me goin' through the night. I pry off the lock on the coalshed door, fill the sacks an' load them on the sled. The snow's six inches deep, sleigh's easy to pull. Even pullin' it three miles is easy.

But while I'm at the coalshed, a chinook blows up from the west. It's suddenly warm. After the first mile, I take my jacket off. I'm sweatin'. Next mile, the snow's become soft an' the sleigh runners are cuttin' through. The pulling's heavy now. I do a lot of fallin' an' slippin'. Third mile home, I'm pullin' a sled with six sacks of coal through patches of mud.

Mountie car picks me up in its headlights.

"Hey, punk! What in hell you got there?" a queen's cowboy hollers at me. "What're you doin' out this time of night?"

"I'm deliverin' coal for the widow Hughes, sir," I say. An' I lean into the rope, pullin' a load that's heavy as the boulders of paradise by now.

"Good boy," says the cop. "Good to see a kid workin' his ass off for a widow! Now get on with it before I nail you for operatin' a transport business with no licence!"

They drive away, an' through the next two hours of night, I'm pullin' the heaviest load of my life. Two years before, my mother had me move a rockpile from the garden into a slough at the bottom of the street. I carried two rocks at a time. It would've taken me ninety years to move those rocks that way.

There's a small metal wagon belonged to a kid called Dinty Maynor halfway down the block. Dinty's in for lunch. Wagon is left on the sidewalk. I nip the wagon an' load it with rocks. I'm big for my age — kids an' their wagons are nothin' to me — I should be loadin' flatdeck trucks. So I pile on the rocks, grab the handle an' go. I pull the wagon about six feet an' all four wheels fall off. I'm mad. I yank the handle, an' *it* comes off.

Little Dinty Maynor, with a face like pink jello, cried six months over that wagon. I stole tobacco from my old man's pouch, an' sat beside Dinty an' smoked while he cried.

Both of us was eight years old then.

There was another kid, Jiggy Monroe. I'd grown up, gone to work an' come back to town for a visit, but stayin' at the hotel, because my mother had died an' the old man said he'd cut my hands off if I returned. Jiggy was fifteen when I got back. He was curly-haired an' dressed in a white shirt an' blue pants, always the same combination. He grew up on weiners an' sauerkraut, the same punk food I grew up on, except he was built like a dancer, an' I come out lookin' like a brick crapper.

A homegrown kid — but he could give a man the best blow-job to be had between Fort Smith an' the yankee border! The first time he took my anchor in his lips I thought my skull was goin' to pop open. We were both under a spruce in an open field a mile out of town. I remember hearin' meadowlarks somewhere . . . an' a sound, somethin' like a moan, comin' up from the black skin of the earth . . .

He was an artist! He was an angel! His white shirt open at the throat, skin soft as silk! Imagine — a homegrown kid who got that way before he was shavin'!

The first time he blew me, he racked up my legs. I was walkin' like a cowboy with saddle-burn for three days before I could straighten out. A couple of days later, the mounties came to my hotel room an' invited me to pack an' leave town in ten minutes or face a charge of contributin' to juvenile delinquency. But Jiggy Monroe didn't get off as easy. He was caught in the alley back of the poolhall an' rapped with a morals conviction. Into the slammer with him, where the hammerboys of the jock world went to work on him.

When they'd finished with him six months later, his face was all scarred an' there was a wild stare in his eyes I'd never seen before. Wild an' haunted, like a beautiful animal what had got itself caught an' tangled in a mile of snare wire.

"Jiggy — what'd they do to you?" I asks when I see him next.

"They impressed upon me that screwin' for joy was forbiddin. They've convinced me!"

"You're kiddin'!"

"Try to tell me otherwise an' I'll punch you in the mouth!" he said sharply an' walked away.

Jiggy tried to work in small towns around Calgary — first at a service station an' then in a clothing store. But he didn't last in either place. There was too much talk about him.

Next time I heard of him, he'd joined the American army an' gone to fight a war for the yanks in Korea. I had a letter from him from Seoul, describin' how he was spendin' all his time on sick leave in the cathouses of Tokyo.

"Women aren't as much fun — but they keep me out of trouble," he says in his letter. Then he described how he managed to stay sick. Breakin' a leg gettin' out of bed, or another time he burned his hands stealin' gas for a jeep. He never fought. All his time in Korea was spent gettin' better.

I'm in Vancouver promotin' a small fight a couple of years later an' I run into him on Granville. He'd just come back from the war. He'd put on weight on yankee war food. That made me mad, an' I lace into him.

"What the hell's happened to you? You depress me. You look like you could sell used cars, or real estate!"

"It's that noticeable, eh?" That lost, wild look returned to his eyes, but only for a flicker.

"You're gettin' fat, old. Man, you were lightenin' an' rainbows together one time. You made somethin' sing inside me just to see you cross a street!"

"You haven't heard the worst yet." He drops his head an' looks away from me. "Romeo, I'm diseased . . ."

"Diseased?"

"Yeh, I copped it two weeks ago. Went to a bar, then for a walk. It felt good to be back on home soil, to smell the north again. I thought the Orient had milked my balls dry. The last six months were hell. I used to go to a whore house

112

an' recite Walt Whitman to guys restin' up between bangs. The delicacy of my life came to me at such times . . . also, the futility. So I'm walkin' down Hastings. I stop to look at Chinese ivory carvings in a shop window. Beside me is a girl with pigtails, white socks an' a pile of books on her arm. She smiles at me, an' suddenly all the rages come back, like I'd never been away. I'm all set to oblige the world — I feel this extra flesh meltin' off my body, the blood hurtin' my eyes . . ."

"I know the feelin'," I says, "I know the feelin' . . ."

"We both walk, apart at first, then arm in arm. I tell her of death an' bomb craters I've seen. She tells me of Friday choir practice, an' a twenty-fourth of May trip she took to Victoria. We walk a long distance. It gets dark. I love her so I can no longer walk without pain. She says — 'What's wrong?'"

"I tell her . . . She laughs, an' turnin' to me, kisses me. I begin to burn, the flames lickin' up my thighs, over my chest an' face. My mouth tastes like charcoal. I stumble, blind now. We turned into someone's garden, an' finding a dark place under a rhododendron bush . . . we did it . . . divinely, Romeo, like two saints in a wilderness. She had the body of a child. Tiny breasts just comin' into bloom, skin still scented with the sour-sweet odor of the infant."

"How old was she?"

"I don't know. I never asked. After all I'd been through since I saw you, I always came out clean an' refreshed — reborn. Other guys got clap just leavin' camp for coffee."

"Don't tell me the kid gave you a dose!"

"A dose is nothin'. A four day cure cleans it up. This was worse. Siberian cankers an' the sift! I'm so low now I could cry. I don't even know if I'll ever be well again . . ."

I put my arm around him an' we went down the street lookin' for a bar. We got drunk together, but the fat on his face didn't get thinner. In fact, he seemed to puff up more the harder we tried to be happy.

"After all I've done an' lived through, this happens with the last person I love . . . a child," he starts to say. Which was my signal for movin' him on to the next bar, an' the next.

My fighters were in town, livin' in a rundown fleanest of a hotel which still rented rooms for under five bucks a night. As a last resort, I flagged a cab an' took Jiggy over to meet the boys, hopin' it might cheer him. Only two of them were in — an oxhead from Arkansas named Tiny, an' Ripper, an oldtimer from Toronto. Tiny was scheduled to wrestle in the preliminaries.

The room smelled of unwashed clothes an' too much beer. Ripper let us in.

"Yeh, you're just in time, Romeo," Ripper grunted as he showed us in. "We was just gettin' ready to stretch old Arkansas."

Tiny Arkansas was sittin' on the bed, his glasses on an' his enormous belly restin' on his knees. He had a torn tee-shirt on, an' his socks. Bottom half of him had no pants or shorts. I looked at Jiggy, who was frowning, his eyes half-closed.

"Sorry, old buddy," I says to him. "I didn't set this up as a joke."

"I know you didn't," he replied softly.

Ripper sat down on a chair in front of Tiny Arkansas an' lifted a contraption off the floor. It was a hand pump attached to a rubber hose, at the end of which was a glass jar, like a two-quart sealer my mother used for cannin' pickles.

"We was gonna stretch old Arkansas here, but this fuckin' gizmo won't work."

"You grease the neck of the bottle with vaseline, or you won't get an' airlock on the thing," Jiggy said quietly, then went to the window which he threw open. He leaned out to get some air.

"What the hell's that?" I asked.

114

"Hey — that's right. I should've thought of that myself!" Ripper was laughin'. He reached for a Brylcream tube on the dirty table behind him an' applied a coating of hair-grease to the rim of the bottle.

"What is it?" I asked again.

"A cock-stretcher," Jiggy said without turning. "Use it often enough an' you'll end up with a flab hangin' in front of you the size of a deflated football . . ."

"How big's it get when it stands up?" Arkansas asked in a voice which was closer to a bulldog bark than anything human.

"Gimme that!"

I wanted to have a closer look at the thing.

"Enormous the first few times. Then the ruptures heal. The scars close off the blood supply an' it won't stand up any more," Jiggy was talkin' to Arkansas, who wasn't listenin'. I'd picked up the equipment an' had a good look at it. The goddamned thing was a vacuum pump.

"It's like a milkin' machine for a man," I said. "Come on, Arkansas — get it on. Let's pump you up an' see what happens!"

The old wrestler took the jar an' jammed it over his tiny root. Then he leaned back in bed so he could watch the action over his stomach.

"Tiny figures the reason he can't get laid is because for a big man he's got an awful small one. I figured this would help. I got an extra inch out of mine with the pump," Ripper was enthusiastic as hell as he started to work the pump.

"Yah, another inch would help!" the big bellied man was sayin'.

Jiggy turned his face back into the room an' leaned against the windowsill to watch. There was a tired smile on his face. He looked ten years older than when I'd met him a few hours before.

The room was silent now, except for the sound of the

pump quishing as Ripper worked it, slowly at first, then more quickly. Inside the bottle, somethin' was stirrin', as the old sayin' goes.

"Is it the stretcher, or you gettin' it on by yourself?" Ripper asks, pausin' in his work.

"Keep pumpin'! The air's leakin' back in!" Arkansas bellows at him.

I pushed Ripper away an' took over the pump handle myself. I worked that damned thing so fast the cylinder got warm. Suddenly the suction leak sealed, an' I seen Arkansas' eyes bulge as the thing inside the bottle popped open. It didn't get longer, however. It just got thicker.

"Think of a broad, Arkansas! You got to help . . . My arm's gettin' sore!"

But Arkansas wasn't worried. He was laughin'.

"Hey — looky here!" he's pointin' with a finger that's thick as a pitchfork handle. He's propped himself up on his elbows an' starin' over his stomach at the glass jar. I worked the pump faster.

"Slow down, Romeo," he says. "It's startin' to hurt a bit . . ."

"Your cord's too short then. What the hell use is this if what you got there's wired tight?" I says to him. I stopped pumpin' for the thing was gettin' bigger on its own, blooming out in a jerky sort of way. Arkansas was sweatin' with pain, but he was happy.

"Never see it like that before!" he exclaims. "You can hold 'er there! Anythin' bigger's no use to me anyway!"

For half a minute he admired it, his eyes shinin'. As a cock, it was an awful specimen — thick, stubby, with a bend to the left side. I've seen better fixtures on dead horses. But I couldn't disappoint old Arkansas.

"Yep, you got yourself a winner there, Arkansas," I says to him.

"They can keep callin' you Tiny, but you'll know it's

116

not because of that, eh?" Ripper was doin' his best to please his partner.

"Naw, never again."

The old man wiggled to get a better look at his prize. Just then there was a sizzling sound, followed by an obscene raspberry as the rubber hose connectin' the pump to the bottle split. Arkansas sat up an' bent over to see into the bottle. What had been a respectable root a moment before wilted down an' amost disappeared into the folds of skin under his stomach.

Jiggy moved away from the window an' quickly left the room. I followed, an' caught up with him on the street outside the hotel. He was hangin' on to a light post, an' laughin' until the tears were runnin' down his face. I grabbed hold of the same pole an' laughed with him.

An' you know somethin', kid? Under that streetlight the face I seen was of the Jiggy Monroe I knew way back as a young punk before he hit the slammer. He was young again, elegant, a sweet devil glowin' in his dark eyes. His lips full an' red as on the most beautiful woman!

"Hey, Jiggy! You gonna live!" I yells at him.

"Damn right I'm gonna live!" he hollers back at me, liftin' his hand to his lips an' then touching mine.

We were both laughin', dancin' down the street.

In opposite directions . . .

ten

It's almost morning again. How quickly the nights an' days pass, from cradle to the death van. We begin an' end ridin' on wheels. If I was king, I'd make the wheel a thing to worship. Hang used tires around every flagpole an' make the boy scouts stand an' salute it! Bearded old priests would be guys hangin' around garbage dumps full of old truck rims. Wars would be fought between punks loyal to Goodyear inner tubes takin' on savages with Sieberling on their side. Anyone caught pissin' on a car hubcap gets shot without trial!

Why have trials anyway? What's it got to do with justice. It costs money to have a trial — so justice is a commodity that sells the same way as eggs, shoes or half a freezer beef. You pay for what you get. If you don't pay, you get an earful of wind, a kick in the butt an' time in the slammer.

It's all a game with winners holdin' trumps before they enter. If you're poor, or walk with a slouch, or speak with a stutter, you've lost before you make your first move. If you're a man takin' on a broad, you're also beat. Broads an' Indians get all the breaks now. The ones who lost out in the trade-off were Pakistanis. Old age pensioners got things good too — but arthritics still got to beg for money.

When I left my wife, she kept on workin' as a cashier in a supermarket in Calgary. For a while, before I found my feet, I lived with women who were like my wife. Spent a year in Vancouver with a broad called Jennie, who was a cashier in a supermarket. She was stronger than my wife an' a bit rounder, but that's probably because she hadn't had a kid to drain her out. She's makin' good bread, this Jennie, but I always get stuck with rent an' taxi fares. If we go out

119

to eat, I pay, even when it's on my birthday. What she gives me don't cost her nothin', or so she makes it seem.

One day, she goes to a doctor. A doctor who looks after women's problems. She's back at work the same day, but a week later, I get this bill for twelve dollars an' seventy cents.

It's made out to me, so I says to her, "What the hell's this?"

"It's the bill for my examination," she says.

"This geek looks at your twat an' I get charged twelve-seventy — what in hell makes you think I'm payin' for this?"

"You broke it, you fix it," she says an' walks out the door. I had a good laugh about it, but five years later I got thinkin' about it, an' I didn't find it funny at all . . .

Shadows an' lights move across the land. The wind moves them. But never is it the same wind, an' I've never seen the same clouds or swath of sun. Why is that? God spends a lot of time makin' variations on one theme. Seems to me he could do better workin' on makin' a bigger cabbage head, or a fish a man can catch with his hands.

I've got to go out pretty soon. Should have gone seven hours ago, but two guys start talkin' an' before half of what's got to be said is said, the night's gone an' it's another day. Well, what difference does it make, eh? In life, everythin' moves around enough to balance off everythin' else . . . justice, broads, or havin' a friend who'll listen to you.

But this is gettin' too serious. Morning's comin' into the city ridin' white frost. The only warmth left is the love of two, ten or fifty people. The more the better!

I got to tell you about women, kid, or you'll always be an animal, an' that's no good to you or anybody. There's different kinds of screwin'. I know guys who do it out of boredom, others for duty. Then there's small guys who do it to tall broads out of vengeance — the one-shot slam-bam-thank-you-ma'am hobos who plant a scrawny kid like themselves inside a big woman every time they get a chance. Screwin' out of love is so rare I can't talk about it. I only seen it explained to me in the ballet I seen last night, an' that don't help you or me much. The closest thing to that I know is screwin' out of pity. To find that, you've got to have pity for everythin' that lives. You can laugh at life, punch it in the teeth, kiss it an' beat it in the ass. But at sundown, somethin' in you has to make you stop an' think, an' cry if it helps about what we do an' what is done to us.

There's two sisters that I know — Elizabeth an' Myrna. They've got an apartment in town, overlookin' the river valley. A quiet apartment; rugs on the floor, grey furniture made in Germany, a kitchen with copper pans, two bedrooms an' a bathroom with colored fixtures. Both broads make good money. Elizabeth is a nurse. Her sister's a broadcaster workin' for television. She interviews me one night before a fight.

"Do you enjoy the violence of the ring?" she asks.

"Sure . . ."

"Why?"

"I was raised mean . . . When I was a baby, my mother fed me with a slingshot an' my father . . ."

She turns away an' makes a motion with her hand to stop the filming. Everybody's grinnin': the cameraman, soundman an' joe-boys carryin' cable around the studio. She turns back to me, an' she's not laughin'. Her large brown eyes are lookin' into mine . . . She leans forward, lookin' into my skull. I'm not sure I want a broad lookin' into such places.

"Have you nothing to say?" she asks me in a low voice.

"Lady, I've got a helluva lot to say. But not everythin' I know or wish for can be put into words!" I says to her. She nods, raising an eyebrow . . .

"Do it! Show me what you know — in any language. I'll get out of your way if that's necessary, but prove to me you're awake. That everything around us here has some sense! That death is someplace over there, but we're here, living, moving, maybe even singing!"

Them words were like fire, kid, sputtering on my skin — inside my brain.

"No, you sit there!" I says. An' I get up in that pokey little room with lights everywhere burnin' out my eyes. All this body of mine's been trained to do is fight for a payin' public. I can sing, an' because I can sing, I can hear music in my head. Sometimes it's soft an' distant, like a thousand flutes playin' in a valley twenty miles away. Other times it's like drums of war beatin' so loud my ears ring an' my jawbones ache. This night, I'm hearin' both. I spit in my hands an' grin at her, an' she's on her feet now an' circling back into the shadows, watchin' me, but her eyes alive an' on fire. The lackeys in the room are starin' like zombies, but they don't matter. I don't see them anymore.

All I see through the lights an' darkness is what I might've been, what we all might've been, a burnin' dart, fallin' through the sky. Fire an' ice. My arms stretching out collectin' dreams an' dust. Then with my hands, I make a world. When it's made, I stamp on it with my foot, an' it don't fall apart. To the sound of flutes, I make trees an' mountains. Then the drums start to hammer, an' I'm down on my knees, makin' a woman. I'm singin' to her as I make her of the softest mud I can find. I'm singin' to her as I take my clothes off an' mount her. I'm still singin' as I lean back on my elbow an' watch the children we've made run away, punchin' an' pushin' at each other as they go to take over the fields an' mountains I made. A few have made themselves slip-willow whistles an' are playin' music. A lot more have picked up clubs an' are cornerin' land, broads an' hilltops from which they can control things. I laugh, an' the woman I've made laughs . . .

I'm in Myrna's apartment later that night. We've had

each other twice, an' are now sittin' in the kitchen, slowly drinkin' wine. She's only wearin' a dressin' gown. Her skin is dark an' hot. Elizabeth, dressed in white like a nun, is makin' coffee. Both broads have the same face, the same bodies. But there's a difference.

In Elizabeth's bedroom, there's a picture of a man on the dressing table. A boy-man, curly-haired an' squintin' as if he'd just woke up an' was lookin' into bright light.

"He drowned in a sea-dive exploring marine specimens. A stupid death. Faulty equipment an' bad support staff. We were very happy together . . ." she tells me, then her voice trails off. She stretches out beside me, her head fallin' back on my arm. The young widow waitin' for the hurt to go. I reach up an' turn the boy-man's face to the wall. Then I turn out the light . . .

Two sisters, two halves of one woman. Myrna risin', Elizabeth fallin'. In the heat of things a man an' woman do together, one laughs, the other cries, her face turned away.

For Myrna I dance an' sing, for she's out to draw all the juices from a man through every open window — the eyes, ears an' mouth. With Elizabeth, I'm prayin' inside me, I'm lamentin', for everything which leaves me to go to her goes to die. I can't have one without the other, so I screw them both out of pity.

It isn't as bad or as good as it sounds, kid. I don't know how it sounds to you. Maybe you're too young to understand. So I'm just tellin' you so you'll remember . . .

Now call me a cab. I'm goin' over to see them. What use is a life if you can't do some good with it? Who'll cry for you when you die?

I've known guys who don't care, but that's another story. We're both feelin' pretty good right now, so let's not worry about them.

Call me a cab . . .